Formerly

SHARK
GIRL

Formerly

SHARK
GIRL

KELLY BINGHAM

JUN   2013

CANDLEWICK PRESS

Copyright © 2013 by Kelly Bingham

First edition 2013

Library of Congress Catalog Card Number 2012952049
ISBN 978-0-7636-5362-0

13 14 15 16 17 18 BVG 10 9 8 7 6 5 4 3 2 1

Printed in Berryville, VA, U.S.A.

This book was typeset in Granjon.

Candlewick Press
99 Dover Street
Somerville, Massachusetts 02144

visit us at www.candlewick.com

*This book is for all the readers who asked
for more of Jane's story. Without you, this book
would not have been written.*

Listening

Over a year ago,
I went into the ocean
with my whole life
planned out, expected,
casually tucked between pages
of a sketchbook.

That all changed in a heartbeat.
A shark
took my arm
and nearly took my life.

"You could have died.
Instead, you are here. You have time to find out why.
You have your whole life to discover
and rebuild."
That's what Mel,
my therapist back in the hospital,
once told me.

When news shows played that awful video
that somebody happened to take
the moment I was torn apart in the water,
everyone said it was a miracle,
a miracle I came out of that coma
and only lost an arm.

"You were spared for a reason,"
many people told me,
strangers who sent letters, cards,
and teddy bears.
"It was not your fate
to die that day," some speculated.
Others said, *"God has plans for you."*

Okay, God.
Or Fate.
Or the Miracle Worker of Hapless Swimmers.
What is your plan for me?
What am I meant to do?
Please.
Tell me.

I'm all ears,
though as you can see,
half-armed.

Senior Year

Mom drops me off in front of school.
"This year is going to go by *way* too fast,"
she predicts glumly.

I walk up the steps into school,
the sounds of my classmates
like old, familiar music.
Inside, I say hello to people I pass
and search for my friends.
A new backpack is light on my back,
and my spirits?
Well, let's just say that compared to last year,
my spirits are high.

Last year, the first day of school
was the stuff of nightmares. Filled
with stares and whispers from everyone
laying eyes on my amputated arm
for the first time since that awful video
hit the air. Last year,
I was so nervous about the first day of school
that I puked before I even left the house.
Today? Today I am filled with gratitude
that *that* day is behind me. Forever.

"Jane!" Angie squeals, her arms wide. "Hey!"
Though I've seen my friends over the summer,

it's always a big deal to see them *here,*
our first day. And this year is an even bigger deal.
This year, we are seniors.

"Hi, Angie." I hug her one-armed,
as Trina, Elizabeth, and Rachel
emerge from the crowd. "Hey, everyone!"
Among hugs, chatter, our slamming locker doors,
the countdown of our last year together begins.
Next year the first day of school will be
in a college somewhere. With unfamiliar faces,
new hallways, and big spaces.
My friends will be scattered to the wind,
each on her own path, her own dream, and all of us
separated for the first time since third grade.
It's too scary to even *think* about.
So for now?

For now, I don't.

In Between

The tweezers slip from my fingers,
clatter to the scuffed floor.
Matthew, my lab partner,
picks them up and lays them on the table.

I whoosh a tight breath,
resisting the urge to scream.
This is one of those cases
where my left hand can't do the delicate work
I want it to. "You do it," I tell Matthew,
amazed that I sound cheerful.
Matthew pauses. "Are you sure?"

"Yes." I gesture
toward the lifeless frog, stretched
before us, belly up on a small plank.
"We don't have much time left."
Matthew, nice guy that he is,
hesitates again, so I assure him,
"It's fine. I'll watch."
And I do.
I watch Matthew poke tentatively
at the gray innards of the frog
as around us, our classmates do the same,
some of them groaning in disgust.
This is the part of having one arm
that I never get used to.

Having to be the watcher sometimes
instead of the doer.

Later,
in art class,
I wait.

I wait as everyone
stretches canvases over wooden frames
and nails them into place.
I wait until my favorite teacher of all time,
Mr. Musker, has a free moment
and can nail my canvas for me
while I hold it in place,
because I can't hammer nails
in a precise manner with my left hand.
And believe me, I've tried.
I never *wanted* to nail things before
that shark attack.
But now? Now I do.

When Mr. Musker finishes my canvas,
everyone else is well under way, painting.
As is often the case, I am last.

I tell myself it doesn't matter.
I tell myself it could be worse.
I tell myself that I will get there.
I will.

Dipping my brush into the red paint,
I wonder
how much longer
I will tell myself these things
before
I believe them.

Plans

"It's September, guys," Angie reminds us.
"We have to get our college applications in *soon*."
Rachel rolls her eyes. "Not till November, Angie."
"Plenty of time," Trina adds. She shivers.
"It's kind of scary."
We nod as though this is the first time she's said this.
The fact is, we *all* said this a hundred times this summer.

"I've decided to apply to Cal State," Angie says.
"But I don't know what I want to study yet."
Elizabeth stares. "Then why apply *there*?
It's so expensive."
Angie gives her a pitying look. "Because
that's where *Scott* is going."

We groan. Scott is Angie's boyfriend.
"Sounds like a solid plan," Rachel says drily.
"My first choice is San Diego. To study business.
But I'm applying to other schools, too,
in case they don't take me."
Elizabeth sips at her milk. "Pharmacology,"
she reminds us. "But I'm going to wait a semester."

I pick at my salad.
No one asks me about school.
I've already told them my plan,
if you can call it that.

Since I can't decide between a future in nursing
or art, I plan to apply to both kinds of schools.
And go from there.

I know. I get it. At some point
a decision will have to be made.
But I'm not ready to make that decision.
And at the rate I'm going,
feeling devoted to one thing one day,
and the other thing the next,
I'm starting to wonder
if I ever will be.

Mom says this is part of being a teen.
She says this is all natural.
She says I'll get there.

Mom's usually right about a lot of things.
But what if this time
she's not?

Two Fingers

Push with two fingers.
Not ten. Not even five.
When you perform CPR on an infant,
two fingers are all you need.

"Excellent," the instructor tells me.
She watches me press, count,
then gently puff into the tiny plastic mouth
of the CPR dummy —
the one resembling a baby,
its plastic arms stiff,
its mouth reeking of antiseptic.
"Very good," she tells me,
and I glow inside.
This is something I can do,
and do well, and it *matters*.

I'm here on a Saturday because
when I was recovering in the hospital,
I found out what it's like to suffer
and what it's like to have people
ease that suffering. I wondered
if I could do it, if *I* could make a difference.
I even began to wonder
if I could become a nurse.

Now I volunteer at the hospital
and am taking all the first-aid training I can.
I hope it will help me figure out
if medicine is right for me.

The instructor helps the girl next to me,
who tries to puff air into the dummy
while holding her hair out of the way.
"You need to put your hand here,"
the instructor tells her.
She demonstrates the proper hold.
Chest compressions, puffs of air,
watch the chest rise and fall,
because if it doesn't,
you are dealing with a blocked airway.
Check for a pulse.
The girl, still holding her hair, is confused.
I think how I don't have two hands
yet I'm doing a better job than she is.

I shove that thought from my head
because it's dangerous.
"Never have a chip on your shoulder,"
Lindsey, my former nurse,
has told me many times.

Besides, when we practice the Heimlich maneuver,
Ms. Hair becomes my partner.
After a startled glance at my prosthetic arm,
she consents to being the choking victim.
Then we switch.
She does the Heimlich better than me.
But still. I can *do* it.
I may not be able to dissect frogs
or nail a canvas,
but I can save a life.
You hear that?
I can save a life.

"Good job," the girl says, coughing.

At home I tape the small certificate
over my desk,
next to the latest pencil sketch of Mabel, my dog,
and a painting of Michael's truck,
which I run my five fingers over.

I hope I never have to perform CPR
or the Heimlich on anyone. *Ever.*
But if I do, I'm ready.

I'm ready.

Stepping Out

"Ready?" Rachel asks,
walking into my room.
I hear her pause. "What are you doing?"
I straighten. "Nothing."
Her eyes meet mine.
"You're using tweezers
to pick up earrings," she says.
"You call that nothing?"
I stretch my neck a little.
"Just an experiment."
"To see if you can pick up your jewelry
with tweezers?"

I rise and gather my things.
Rachel and I are headed out for iced coffee.
"Well, I had some trouble the other day
in science, with the tweezers
and dissecting the frog. So I thought . . ."
Rachel shakes her head.
"You thought you'd teach yourself
how to use those tweezers with your left hand,
so that the next time you are called upon
to dissect a frog, you'll be ready?"
"Something like that."

"Well, Jane. One thing about you:
you're not a quitter.

And you *hate* not being able to do something.
Anything."

We grin at each other
as we walk out of my room.
"True. I do hate defeat."
We head out into the bright sunshine,
our purses swinging from our shoulders.
"By the way," Rachel says,
"I brought some brochures from San Diego.
It looks fantastic.
It would be awesome to go to college there."

Hearing Rachel say *go to college*
is like a sharp nudge in the ribs.
Maybe once we're separated,
things won't ever again
be this easy between us,
me and my best friend.

The thought makes the sunshine slip,
for just a moment,
behind a smothering cloud
of gray.

Letter from Wendy Stewart
Editor, *Valley Magazine*

Dear Ms. Arrowood,

My name is Wendy Stewart, and I am the editor of
Valley Magazine, *which is devoted to stories of life in*
southern California. You may recall we ran a piece about
you soon after your horrible shark attack. Though you were
not available for comment then, we have our fingers crossed
that you will grant us an interview now. We plan to write a
follow-up segment to your extraordinary story for our next
issue and would love to be able to quote you directly. Would
you grant us a small amount of your time?

If you agree to the interview, we'll send our photo-
grapher to Santa Clarita to take photos of you at home and
at school. We would also like to take pictures of you at Point
Dume State Beach, as close as we can estimate to the spot
where the attack happened. Out of curiosity, have you been
back to the ocean since this happened?

The reason we want to write this follow-up story is
because many readers have written to us and asked us for
one, Ms. Arrowood. People remember you and want to
know how you are now, how you have fared since the loss of
your arm and nearly the loss of your life. People remember
that striking video and your story. Won't you please grant us
an interview? I have enclosed our contact information and
hope to hear from you soon.

Also, one of our staff was at Santa Clarita Hospital for a minor injury last month. She spotted you working there as a volunteer. You came to her room and took her tray, and she said you were very kind! She said when she engaged you in conversation, you mentioned you were thinking of becoming a nurse. Would you please confirm this?

Best wishes,

Wendy Stewart

Letter from Jane Arrowood
Santa Clarita, California

Dear Ms. Stewart,

Thank you for contacting me. I am very appreciative of the interest of your readers. However, I do not wish to do an interview. Thank you just the same. As for confirming that I work at the hospital, yes, I do. And yes, I am considering nursing for my future, as well as many other possibilities. Thank you.

Sincerely,
Jane Arrowood

Darkness and Light

Late-afternoon sunlight illuminates
squares of windowpanes in the art classroom.
Mr. Musker and I pore over a book about Rembrandt,
one of the world's greatest painters.
"Study his use of darkness and light," Mr. Musker says.

I linger over *The Blinding of Samson* and *Danäe*.
Shafts of light, cloaks of darkness,
compositions of color and structure
that funnel your eye exactly where he wanted.
"Wow" is all I can say,
and it's not enough. Through the ages,
how many people have said "Wow"
about Rembrandt? How many people
stood before *The Anatomy Lesson of Dr. Nicolaes Tulp*
and said too little
because there were no words
big enough?

"Rembrandt's personal life was a story in its own right,"
Mr. Musker says, adjusting his glasses and turning a page.
"He lost all his children except for one.
They each died at very young ages.
Then his wife died.
He took up with the nurse hired to care for his son.
They had a child together,
and the poor woman was banned from the church.

Later she passed away and he took up with his maid.
I'd say Rembrandt wasn't big on being lonely."

"Oh." I take that in.
Mr. Musker continues.
"He also spent too much. On weird, wild things.
Art collections, mostly. Suits of armor.
He died a poor man and was buried in an unmarked grave."
I stare once more at a self-portrait,
Rembrandt with a Broad Nose,
imagine the hand behind the brush,
the dark, narrowed eyes.
What did he think about at night, lying awake?
Was he unhappy? Did he dwell on his lost children?
Did he see the goodness in his work?

"He was also an art teacher," Mr. Musker says.

"A teacher? Just like you."

Mr. Musker laughs. The sunlight through the window
glints on his thin gray hair.
He has a nice smile, crinkly and catching.
It makes our after-school sessions on Mondays
all the more fun.
"I'm not sure I'd compare myself to Rembrandt,"
he says. "My work hardly compares. Besides,

I doubt Rembrandt ever taught anyone about pottery
or string art or mosaics."

Student artwork hangs on the walls around us.
And some of Mr. Musker's paintings and drawings, too.
Trees, landscapes, a busy and joyous sketch of his young
daughter,
and a painting that is haunting . . .
a white house on a dark night,
with trees and a sliver of a moon,
shadows deep under the porch,
and something oppressive about it,
like a coming storm.
"I think your work is fantastic," I say.
Mr. Musker pats me on the back.
"Thank you, Jane. And right back at you."
He closes the book.
"Take it home for a while."

"Thank you." I unzip my book bag.
Without being asked, Mr. Musker
pushes the book into the bag for me,
followed by my sketchbook and notes.
"I'm so pleased with the progress in your art," he says.
"Your determination is paying off. Do you see it?"
"Not really," I say, hating to disappoint him,
which I do, because he droops a little.

"Well, you are a perfectionist, Jane,
and it's understandable that you're not satisfied yet.
I don't have to tell you,
but I'll tell you anyway:
keep working on it."
"Okay."
"And I do like the piece you are planning to enter
in the contest."
"Me, too. I like it . . . for now.
But I can do better. I hope."
"All right, then. See you later."

For a minute, I see this wonderful art teacher
who has taught me so much over the last four years
as a dad —
a friendly dad who scoops up his small daughter
when he comes home at night,
tickles her, hugs her,
and shows her how to color with crayons.
He wouldn't mind
if her small hands snatched at his glasses.

I want to say something to him,
some words of gratitude
for all he has taught me over the last four years.
For his encouragement and patience.
I want to tell him how much it means.

But all I can come up with is:
"See you, Mr. Musker.
And thank you."

Words that are too small
because there are no words
big enough.

In the Lines

At the hospital, I help Candy,
a little girl recovering from an appendectomy,
color a giant poster.
"Are you sure you want me to do this?"
I ask her again. "It's your poster, after all."

Her tongue sticks out sideways
as she colors the green bucket
in the beach scene before us.
"I'm sure," she says in her tiny voice.
"I want this done by the time Mom
gets here. I need you to help me."

I choose a pink crayon. "For the starfish?"
She shakes her head. "Use orange instead."

I switch crayons. "I like the colors you've chosen."
She smiles. "Thank you." Then she gets stern.
"Stay in the lines, okay? Or at least try to."
I nod seriously. "Okay."

She starts to hum,
a small happy sound that fills the air.
When we finish the poster just in time,
Candy's radiant smile
gives me one of my own.
I fetch her an extra pillow

and close the door to the room
as she and her mother cuddle in a big chair.

It's a good thing this job is volunteer.
I can't imagine accepting one single cent
for spending time
coloring
with Candy.

Brooding

In science class on Monday,
Mr. Veckio hands back our quizzes.
Let's just say I didn't do well. At all.
A black cloud settles over my head.
Have I mentioned that science
is my absolute worst subject? I barely passed last year.
And the year before that.
When Mr. Veckio drones on and I remain confused,
my mood only gets worse.
This spring, I'll apply for financial aid
for college. I'll apply for scholarships.
How many scholarships will be awarded
to someone with horrendous grades in science?
Particularly for nursing school, which looks *heavily*
at that stuff?

When the bell rings,
I can't wait to get out of there.
If I could, I would walk out of my skin
and leave it lying in a puddle on the floor.
Maybe then, some of this weight
would roll off my shoulders
taking that black cloud with it,
and let me breathe again.

Decisions

"College," Mrs. Guiano says cheerfully,
placing her glasses on the end of her nose.
"A big decision." She peers at the page.

The guidance counselor's office
is crammed with posters and books.
Four brochures are spread out across
Mrs. Guiano's desk. I point to them.
"I've got it narrowed down
to these four. Two nursing schools
and two art schools. My applications are ready."
Mrs. G. raises her eyebrows. "Already? It's only October.
Good for you. Most people wait until the last minute."

"I'm ready now," I lie. Who's ever ready for this?
"Everyone wants them by Thanksgiving anyway.
I'll send them all in next month.
Then I can just sit back and wait to hear."
"And when you hear?" Mrs. Guiano asks kindly.
"Then what?"
I blow out my breath. "Easy —
if only one school takes me, then I go *there*."
She laughs, reaches across the desk, and squeezes my hand.
"And if all four schools accept you. Then what?"
I find myself stuck in a shrug.
I straighten up. "I don't know," I admit.
"Nursing or art? I can't decide."

Mrs. Guiano folds up the brochures.
"I think you'd be outstanding at both.
You're smart. You're caring. You're creative.
I haven't seen you in action at your hospital job,
but I sure have seen your artwork. You're fantastic."

Even with my new limitations? I almost ask.
But I don't. What do I expect Mrs. G.
to say to *that*? But still.
The question circles my mind,
as constant as time.
Before that shark took my arm,
I *was* a fantastic artist. I admit it. Now?
Because I'm *still* adjusting to drawing with my left
hand,
I'm only good. Not *fantastic*.
And maybe not even good enough
to get into art school,
let alone make a living at it.
As for nursing?
If I do that, it's because I want
to give back. To help.
To be there for someone in need.
But—can I do that with only one arm?
Seems that both careers call to me,
yet both might be just out of reach.

"So the question remains," Mrs. Guiano says,
offering me her candy jar. "Which will you choose?"
I select a bright lump. "Lemon. Definitely."

She laughs. "I'll take that as another
'I don't know.'" She hands back the brochures.
"Lucky for you, you have plenty of time to decide."

We stand up as the bell rings.
She's right. It's only September.
I won't even hear back from these schools until March.
Seven months is *plenty* of time to decide
what you want to do with the rest of your forever.
Right?

Wrong. But either way, the wheels are in motion.
Now all I have to do is keep moving.

At Your Doorstep

"You know I'm always here,"
Mrs. Guiano says. "Literally.
I may as well have my mail sent here.
Come see me anytime you want."

I can't help grinning back at her.
"Thanks." I turn to leave, my unmade decision
settling back into its worn groove in my psyche.
Which path, Jane? Which path?
The worry and wonder are like terriers,
nipping at my heels. This decision — it feels so huge.
It feels so *important.* You know *why* it feels like that?
Because it *is.*

"Hey, Jane," Mrs. Guiano calls from her doorway.
I turn back. "Yes?"
She points at me as she backs into her office.
"I'm jealous of you, you know."

I laugh in disbelief. "Why?"
She leans against the doorjamb.
"Oh, honey. To have those choices to make.
Baby, the world is at your doorstep.
And you don't even know it.
But believe me. It is. I'd give anything
to be able to start all over and make the choices
you get to make this year."

I consider this as the halls fill with kids
rushing off to classrooms right and left.
It just goes to show. As much as you may think
your life is a mess, well —
your mess might be someone else's envy.
"Mrs. Guiano?" I ask.
"If you *could* go back and make those choices
all over again, would you do anything different?"

Her smile and her reply are immediate.
"Nope. I wouldn't change a thing."

Mulling that over, I head to class.
I hope that years from now,
I can look back
and say the same thing
that she just did.

It's Personal

Ms. Edmonds, our English teacher,
asks, "What did everyone think
about the main character
having a bucket list?"
Nathan raises his hand. "I didn't like it."
Ms. Edmonds cocks an eyebrow.
"Can you tell us why?"

"The whole idea of a bucket list
is weird," Nathan answers.
Elizabeth interjects, "No, it's not.
It's just a way of saying 'goals,' really.
What's wrong with setting goals for yourself?"
Emily smacks her gum. "His goals were *stupid*."

"Who are we to say they're stupid?"
I ask. "They were *his* goals, not ours."
Emily rolls her eyes. "One of them
was to eat a pizza on the beach.
That's not exactly *profound,* is it?"
Mrs. Edmonds steps in. "Goals and desires
don't have to be profound to be meaningful."

"Besides, a bucket list is personal,"
Elizabeth adds. "You wouldn't go around
showing it off to everyone.

So what difference does it make if the goals
are small or large, or sound weird?
No one else is going to see them."

"I'm glad you all have an opinion on this,"
Ms. Edmonds says. "Because today
we are going to write our *own* bucket lists."

There is a small groan from the back.
Ms. Edmonds begins writing on the board.
"You must write at least ten goals
that you want to accomplish
in a specific time period.
You don't have to show this to me.
I am putting you on the honor system.
This is something you can do for *you*.
Think about it.
This may actually mean something
if you want it to."

As if my mind has been waiting
for this opportunity, my left hand
begins scribbling as fast as it can,
which is not very fast. I watch
the list unfold,
as though watching a movie.
Well. What do you know?
I have goals.
Some of them I am working toward,

and some I just now formed.
Seeing them written out
makes me realize:

I have a lot
of work to do.

Bucket List for Senior Year

1. Apply to nursing school and art college.
2. Choose one or the other.
3. Become fully certified in CPR, first aid, and triage.
4. Enter the school art competition.
5. Win the school art competition.
6. Qualify for and enter the West Coast Wings art competition.
7. Win the West Coast Wings art competition.
8. Go to prom.
9. Bake a wedding cake.
10. Save a life.

The Beginning

Justin and I stand in his bedroom,
contemplating the small sketch
taped to the center of the large white wall before us.
"I don't get it," Justin says. "How are you
going to take that little drawing
and turn it into a mural on this big wall?"
I lay my arm across his thin shoulders.
"I'm going to have you help me, of course."

He laughs, then walks over to study the sketch.
Justin has a fake leg, but you'd never know it.
That's how we met, Justin and I. In the hospital.
He lost his leg in a car crash at the same time
I lost my arm to a shark. Though Justin is a lot younger
than I am, he is one of my best friends. And honestly?
He's an inspiration. Justin doesn't dwell on his lost leg.
He is too busy living life.

"First," I tell him,
"We'll transfer that sketch onto the wall.
Then we'll be ready to paint."
Justin's dog, Spot, sniffs my shoe. Justin asks,
"But *how* do we transfer the drawing onto the wall?"

I lay a piece of graph paper over the sketch Justin has directed:
a sunny park scene with grass, trees, fields of people
playing soccer,

and children playing with a dog that looks a lot like Spot.
"See how the graph paper
divides the drawing into squares?"
Justin nods. I go on. "We'll draw a really big graph
on your wall. Then we'll refer to this sketch,
one square at a time.
We copy what's in each small square
over to each big square
in the wall. When you break it down into these small
squares,
it makes it easier to transfer the entire thing over.
See what I mean?"

He nods, though a little slowly. "I think so."
I point to the graph. "We just draw one box at a time.
It will work. Trust me."
He nods again, "I trust you."

That's one of the things I love about Justin.
He has more trust than I do, that's for sure. In himself,
his family, and his friends. In life. The truth?
I envy that about him.
"Let's get started," I tell him, picking up the ruler.
Picking up his own ruler, Justin stands by my side.
Together, we begin.

Sunday

Hey, Sis. I found this by the computer. Your "bucket list"?

Michael! That's *private*!

Well, try not leaving it out in *public,* then. *Sheesh.*

You *wrote on it*!

Cute, huh?

"Number eleven: Become the left-handed arm-wrestling champion of the universe." *No,* it's not *cute.* And you shouldn't have even read it!

How can I resist anything titled "Bucket List"? Besides, if it's any consolation, I like what you've got going there. Some very nice goals.

Go ahead. There's a zinger coming.

I particularly like the way "Go to prom" comes before "Save a life." Nice priorities.

Michael. I hate you. Very much.

No, you don't. I saved your life, remember?

Of course I remember, you moron.

Touchy, touchy.

They are not listed in order of priority, okay? They're
just . . . things I want to do this year. Some of them are
more realistic than others. It's not like I want to be in
the *position* to save a life. I guess I'd like to know that if I
had to . . . I could. You know?

I do, Jane. I see you taking all these medical classes and
doing your time at the hospital. I see how much you care
about this nursing thing. And I'm just kidding, anyway.

Really?

Really. I think you'd make a *fine* wedding cake.
Chocolate, I hope?

Isn't it time for you to head back to the dorms now?

Yep, I was just leaving. After I find my laundry. See you
around, Jane.

Bye.

Thank Goodness

I did not put that one extra thing
on my bucket list for senior year,
the one thing
that is too private to even write down
and see in stark black
words.

Michael would have said something awful
if he'd seen it.

All of my friends
have already had one.
Not me.
I may not have written it down,
but in my head? My heart?
It's there, on the list:

My first kiss.

Star of the Month: What Ever Happened to . . . ?

This month, our segment goes to Jane Arrowood, a high-school student from Santa Clarita. You may remember Jane as the 15-year-old who was attacked by a shark at Point Dume two summers ago. The attack was caught on tape by an anonymous beachgoer. Jane lost most of her right arm due to her injuries from the shark attack. She nearly died from the trauma and was in a coma for several days. Throughout her recovery period, Jane has been notably reluctant to be interviewed and facts about this young lady are hard to come by.

But many of our readers have asked about her, so here is what we know: We did contact Ms. Arrowood and ask for a full interview, but she declined. However, sources tell us that Ms. Arrowood is doing remarkably well and has resumed leading the full, normal life of a high-school senior. She attends SCHS and will graduate this spring. She is said to be friendly, popular, and well liked. And best of all, Jane seems to have taken her personal experience and transformed it into good: She did confirm that she now volunteers at Santa Clarita Hospital and that she intends to become a nurse in the future! We applaud Ms. Arrowood for this decision. Surely

she will bring a great deal of personal experience and empathy to her future patients.

We wish Ms. Arrowood the very best in her future, and we are confident she will go far in life, having demonstrated a great deal of will and determination already.

Hats off to Jane Arrowood, our *Valley Magazine* Star of the Month!

Letter from Wendy Stewart
Editor, *Valley Magazine*

Dear Ms. Arrowood,

I hope you had a chance to read the article we wrote about you for our publication, Valley Magazine. *I wanted to share with you that we have had a* lot *of follow-up mail from our readers. I will forward it all along to you.*

Many readers have asked if you'll write a book about your experience. Some wonder if you'll ever do a TV interview. Many have commented that they'd like to meet you someday. And overwhelmingly, readers tell us that you are an inspiration to them.

I just wanted to share that and to remind you that the door is always open here at Valley Magazine *should you decide you'd like to be heard. We would be glad to do an interview with you at any time.*

Thank you, and best of luck!
Wendy Stewart

Little to Big

The graph stretches across the expanse
of Justin's bedroom wall. Michelangelo
did not work harder on the Sistine Chapel
than I did on making that graph.
Justin and I fill in the squares one by one.
"Little squares to big squares," I tell him.
"But it's just like I told you.
One square at a time. That's all.
Try to look at it one square at a time."

We work a few minutes. Then:
"I can't do this," Justin says,
putting down his pencil.

I stare down at him from my ladder,
shocked. This is the first time
I've *ever* heard Justin say such a thing.
"What are you talking about?" I ask.
He gestures. "I'm messing it up.
My drawings are all crooked."

I climb down the ladder, well aware
of the frustration in seeing your drawings
come out crooked. It *is* maddening.
But this "can't" stuff? From Justin? *No way.*

"The only part that is not right
is this line here," I tell him,
pointing to the top part of a dog,
where he's inverted one long line.
"This part is upside down," I tell him.
"It makes it look like the entire drawing is a mess,
but it really isn't. It's fixable. Just one adjustment.
Like this. See?" I erase the line and draw it properly.
Magically, the dog's form emerges
from the previously lumped-up mess.

Justin blinks. "Oh." He picks up his pencil again.
I see pep returning to that face that I know so well.
"And the ear goes here?" He tentatively scratches
at the wall. I put my hand over his and guide
his pencil strokes. "Yes. But more triangular.
Like that. Get it?"

He nods and begins drawing more boldly.
I watch and encourage, and when we reach
the patch of sunflowers in the corner,
Justin falters again.
"I'm not sure how to draw that,"
he says. So once again, I take his hand
and guide him through it. Together,
we draw long stems, giant blossoms,
and sunny centers. Justin listens to my advice,
and by the time the last flower is done,

he's drawing the petals all by himself,
exactly to scale.

"Excellent!" I tell him, and he beams.
I pick up my pencil and climb the ladder again.
"Time for clouds in the sky."

"I want to do one," Justin says eagerly.
I laugh and climb back down. "Okay,
but I'm going to hold on to you, just to be safe."
He climbs the few steps of the ladder,
and I grip the base of it, keeping it steady.
While he sketches
I look up at him
and feel a flush of happiness.

Justin
is reaching for the clouds.

Discovery

As darkness falls, I sit down to the computer.
I want to study Rembrandt's earliest self-portrait
and look for more medical classes in town.
That's when I find it.
Totally by accident.
It just *pops up,*
already in the browser window.
I guess Mom left it there by mistake.
It's a site — a *dating* site —
where "mature singles gather
to meet, greet, talk and . . . ?"
It promises *"complete compatibility,"*
"no pressure, no gimmicks,"
and *"people just like you, looking for romance."*

In the photos, women Mom's age laugh.
They wear bright, silky clothes and
have clean, shiny hair, and the men
they lean upon gaze at them adoringly.
Everyone is discovering their *"soul mate"* and *"best friend."*

A quick click or two, and there's Mom's in-box —
full
of messages
with headings like, *"Hello there!"*
and *"Fred Watson has sent you a WAVE!"*
and *"Dinner on Friday?"*

There's even one that says
"NEED A FOOT MASSAGE?"

Good grief.
What has Mom
gotten herself into?

And Why?

Okay, maybe I know *why.*
Mom is single.
Maybe she's lonely.
However. This dating site?
So tacky.
I mean . . . *a foot massage?*

My hand hovers over the mouse,
poised to click on her in-box,
to further invade her privacy, and I don't care —
I'm going to see if she answered any of these men.
Did she mention that she has two children?
Did she mention that one of them is the Shark Girl?

Then
the front door bangs open.
Mom calls, "Jane?
Can you help me carry in the groceries?"

In a panic, I nearly knock over my glass of water.
Pressing buttons, trying to cover my tracks,
I somehow turn the entire computer off.
I hurry out to greet her
and pick up a sack bulging with food.

"How are you, sweetie?" she asks.
Her shoulders sag. She's tired,

she's had a long day at work,
and she moves like her feet hurt,
sliding the bags of groceries to the floor.

"I'm fine, Mom. Sit down.
I already have dinner in the oven.
Spinach lasagna."
She kisses my cheek.
"You're my best daughter," she tells me.

Swallowing guilt,
I head into the kitchen,
put away carrots, potatoes,
cereal, and bread —
her words,
her face,
and her secret
heavy

in my heart.

Science and Pain

I take out pen and notebook and fix my eyes
on the prize: peptides and their formations.
That's today's science lesson.

But minutes into class,
pain rips through my half-arm.
A pain so intense,
I can't breathe.
The pain dulls, swells, and throbs wildly.
It's like someone is twisting
a white-hot corkscrew
straight into the end of my stump.

One, two, three, breathe in, hold,
I say to myself,
doing the deep-breathing exercises
I was taught for pain management.
Management for the phenomenon
called phantom limb pain.
That's when you experience agony like this,
like someone is torturing the part of your arm
that you don't even have anymore.

But this is different from phantom limb pain.
The burning ratchets up a notch,
then dulls into a steady crackle.
Three, two, one, breathe out.

I pant, in a private abyss of agony,
as Mr. Veckio drones on, sketching formulas
on the blackboard. He says something,
and kids turn pages in their textbooks.
Sweat trickles down my back.

After a while,
the pain dies down.
Then it's gone.
Relief
does not even begin to describe the result.
Dabbing sweat from my forehead,
I blow out my breath and join the living.
The lesson is over.
The bell rings,
and I've missed it all.
Frustration
does not begin to describe that sensation, either.

Gathering my things,
I hope
it doesn't happen again.

Circles and Squares

In today's after-school art session
with Mr. Musker, I can't get anything right.
And believe me, I'm not being modest.
Even Mr. Musker finally expresses frustration
in the form of a brisk sigh.
"Let's back up a minute," he says.

He removes the canvas from my desk
and replaces it with a pad of heavy paper.
He hands me a Conté crayon, smooth and fat-tipped.
"The basics," he says. "Sometimes you have to
start back at the beginning in order to get unstuck."

He instructs me to draw circles and ovals for ten minutes.
"Seriously?" I look up at him, unsure. Is this punishment?
He must have read my mind, because he laughs.
"This is not a bad thing. This is an exercise, Jane.
I do it all the time when I'm stuck. Go back to square one
and you'll see. Concentrating on simple things can free
your mind to take on the more complicated things later.
Take a deep breath and draw."

And so I do. And as I draw,
the crayon leaving a trail of black
across the white paper,
the circles grow more solid.
The ovals become more fluid.

Something in my hand begins to loosen,
and that looseness slowly spreads
up my arm, all the way to both shoulders,
and into my brain.

Hmm. Isn't this kind of like what I told Justin?
Little to big? One square at a time?
Guess I need to slow down and listen to my own advice.
Sometimes looking too far ahead *can* be overwhelming.
Even for someone who thinks she can handle it.

Mr. Musker returns to my desk and says,
"Squares and rectangles now."
I create a crooked square.
We're wasting time, some part of me screams.
We should be working on a piece I can actually use —
for the art show or a college portfolio.

Go away, I murmur inwardly.
Amazingly, the fretting stops.
Drawing squares and rectangles,
I put my mind to the task at hand.
And I put my faith
in Mr. Musker's methods.

Letter from Marlo
Los Angeles, California

Dear Jane,

Recently I read an update on your story. I'm so glad to hear that your life has resumed being normal and that you have fully recovered from that shark attack.

I am amazed and awed by your experience. Most people can't imagine going through such a terrible thing. And you have overcome it and moved on. I admire that so much. It makes me think even my worst days are nothing to complain about, because, after all, I still have both arms and my good health. Your story has made me appreciate what I have.

I wonder if you feel God has pulled you through this. Clearly He meant for you to live. He must not be done with you here on earth . . . which means He has a purpose for you. Have you found out what that purpose is? Perhaps it was to be an inspiration to people like me. Perhaps it was to be a nurse, as you have chosen to be. What an incredible way to find your calling to help others. I wish you well and thank you for being someone I can look up to.

Your friend,
Marlo

Unexpected

That evening, I'm in the kitchen with Justin.
We're dicing onions for some soup.
The phone rings, and I pick it up. "Hello?"
"Hi. Jane? This is Matthew."
I pause. "Matthew?"
"Yeah. Matthew Singleton.
From science class."
"Oh. Hi, Matthew." I glance at Justin, who
picks up a carrot and nibbles on it.

"What are you doing?" Matthew asks.
I tuck the phone under my chin.
"Um, nothing much."
"I'm studying for the vocabulary quiz tomorrow,"
he says. "I just finished memorizing *momentous*.
We have a long list this week. Have you started?"
I push the onions aside. "No. I'll do it later."
What does he want? Why would he call me?
Matthew clears his throat.
"Do you want to go to the movies this weekend?"

"The movies?" I repeat.
I sound incredulous, even to my own ears.
Justin perks up and puts down his carrot.
Matthew rushes his words. "Not just with me.
A group of us. We're all going on Saturday,
and I wondered if you would like to go.

We might get pizza afterward . . . or ice cream. . . ."
He trails off. Horrified, I realize
he is waiting for me to rescue him.
"Um . . . yes. Yeah! That would be great."
Within minutes, there I am,
hanging up the phone, a group movie date
for Saturday night with Matthew Singleton
on my agenda. Wow. Didn't see that coming.

"You're going to the movies?" Justin asks.
"What are you going to see?"
"Um, I don't know."
Returning to my knife and board,
I notice I begin chopping quite briskly.
A date? I haven't been on a date in . . .
well, I've *never* been on a date, okay?
Yes, I am sixteen. But last year
was the first year I was allowed to date,
and that year turned out to be consumed by
something other than boys and movies.
"Are we almost done?" Justin asks.
"These onions are smelly."
I agree. "You take a break.
Maybe watch some TV? You pick the show."

Justin heads for the living room.
I chop wildly, recklessly.
I never thought of Matthew like that.
Should I? Do I?

It wasn't all that long ago
that I was convinced that no boy
would ever want to be seen with me.
Funny how things change
in ways you never expect.

I slam the knife down
and snatch up the phone again.
A moment like this requires a phone call
to one's best friend.
A moment like this?
You might even call it
momentous.

Phone Call from Jane to Rachel, Midway Through

Rachel: I *love* Matthew! I'm so glad you're going out with him!

Jane: It's a *group* thing, not a date.

Rachel: Okay, Jane. I didn't say you were getting *married.* What are you going to wear? Who's driving? How many people are going?

Jane: Um. I don't . . . know?

Rachel: Is that a question? How can you not know?

Jane: I didn't ask?

Rachel: Hello? Is this the *real Jane Arrowood*? What did you do—hang up the instant he asked, without getting any details? That's not like you. You're normally more . . . bulldoggish.

Jane: Thanks so much. I did hang up kind of fast. I was . . . flustered.

Rachel: Don't worry about it. I bet he was, too. The main thing is you're going.

Jane: I don't know what time. I don't know anything except that it's Saturday. I'm an idiot. How can I have not asked for more details?

Rachel: Well, won't this give you two something to chat about in science class tomorrow?

Jane: Apparently.

Rachel: Ms. Jane Singleton . . .

Jane: This is *Matthew.* I never even thought of him that way. Actually, I haven't thought of *anyone* that way lately.

Rachel: That's because you spent all last year thinking about Max Shannon, the heartthrob who got away.

Jane: Max? I didn't really . . . I mean, I *did,* but . . .

Rachel: Jane, I wasn't crazy about Max like you were, and even *I* still think about him sometimes. This would be a whole other conversation if *he* was the one who asked you out. Wouldn't it?

Jane: Can we get back to the subject?

Rachel: I heard Max went to college in New York.
I heard his girlfriend broke up with him because
she went to school in Utah and didn't want to try the
long-distance thing. Did you hear any of that?

Jane: No.

Rachel: How do I know this stuff and you don't?

Jane: *Rachel.* Back to the date. Do I pay my own way?
Does he pay? How does that all work?

Rachel: Well . . .

Jane: Wait. We'll have to talk about this later. Justin is
here, and I'm ignoring him. I'll call you after dinner.

Rachel: I'll be here.

Jane: Bye!

Max Shannon

Okay. Yes, last year I was a little bit in love
with the school's swim-team star,
Max Shannon.
Silly. It was the crush kind of love,
based on not knowing anything
about someone other than
they are gorgeous and funny and kind
and the one person in the entire school
who did not stare, gawk, or
develop sudden blindness
that awful, awful
first day of junior year,
when I started school with only one arm,
a mountain of news stories,
and one gory, jarring video
piled upon my head, shoulders,
and reputation.

And yeah . . . I still think about him once in a while.

But Max was kind to me —
that's all. He drove me home a few times.
We never exchanged more
than a few minutes of conversation.
He was there, in the same school,
orbiting in a different universe from mine,

then he graduated and disappeared,
and that was that.

But Matthew? Matthew is *real*.
And Matthew wants to take me out.
I can't wait
to see
where this goes.

Back Again

Stab — as though a knife
slips under my skin, savagely slicing.
I gasp and grab my half-arm.
"What's wrong?" Mom asks,
putting her fork down.
I get up from the table,
sweat breaking out across my forehead.
"Just some limb pain," I tell her.
Mom fetches ice.

The cold helps. I lie on the couch,
the ice pack pressed against my stump.
Please don't tell me I'm having a setback,
I think, addressing . . . whom?
I did all this already, okay?
I don't want to do it again.

And the fact is, I'm sort of a baby
when it comes to hurting.
Usually,
like now,
I cry.

Letter from George
Newhall, California

Dear Jane,

I read an update about you in Valley Magazine *a while back, and I keep thinking about you. I always wondered how you were doing, and I'm so glad to hear you are well.*

I can only imagine the tough road you have traveled. I think it's wonderful that you have moved on with your life and not let this one thing drive you down the wrong path. The article mentioned you are planning to become a nurse. That is fantastic. I am sure you will be spectacular at that. Good for you, Jane.

As the magazine said, I bet you will be wonderful at whatever you do in life. You are obviously an exceptional person with a great deal of courage.

Best wishes,

George

Triage, Class One

"You would apply pressure,
like this." The instructor of the triage class,
a birdlike man with the longest
legs I have ever seen
(and, unbelievably, named Mr. Stork),
demonstrates for the class,
pressing a mound of cloth to the fake victim,
who is sprawled on a silver metal table.
All of us watch, take notes,
then put down our pencils and gather
at the front of the room to practice on one another.

This is the first of three triage classes.
I am here, partly, because it helps,
when applying for nursing school,
to have as much training as you can.
But mostly I am here because
I want to be. I want to know
what to do in an emergency.
I want to know how to save a life.
Call me crazy, but this knowledge?
It makes me better. Stronger. Empowered.

"I am handing out injuries,"
Mr. Stork says with a ghoulish grin.
"Break into groups of four, with one person
the victim and everyone else the helpers.

When it's your turn, your fellow students
will assess your injuries and decide what to do about them."
Four of us gravitate nervously together in a clump,
all of us different ages. Some of us are serious, and some,
like the boy behind me, chuckle and shuffle.
"For your group," Mr. Stork says,
handing the boy a slip of paper.

The boy opens it and reads out loud:
"Sucking chest wound.
Severe shortness of breath.
Uneven chest."
He puts the paper in his pocket.
"Man. Sucks to be me."

The boy lies on a spongy blue mat on the floor.
Around us, other groups play out similar scenarios.
I overhear someone say, "Burns and shrapnel on the torso,"
and then everyone bumps shoulders
as we cluster around the red-faced boy,
who lolls his head to one side.
"Don't let me die, okay?" he pleads theatrically,
eyelids fluttering.

We work as one, recalling what we learned
about triaging a sucking chest wound.
"Uneven chest—his lung is probably collapsed,"
I say. "We have to seal the wound."
A gray-haired man with glasses shakes his head.

"Sealing the wound can prevent air from getting in,"
he says. "The guy may suffocate."

Mr. Stork materializes by my side.
"This young lady is right. You need to seal the wound."
We search through the list of items we have to work with.
A lady in a pink sweater grabs a box of Saran Wrap.
"Here!"
We snatch up tape.
I hand scissors to Gray-Haired Man because
cutting with my left hand is not my speediest thing.
Murmuring advice, we watch as he cuts the patch.
"It needs to be much larger than the wound,"
Sweater Lady says, and the man snaps,
"How am I supposed to know how big *that* is?
There's no real wound, in case you haven't noticed."
In the end, he cuts out a piece the size of a fist.
Sweater Lady tapes it down while I hold it in place.
Then we apply a clean bandage, all three of us working
together.

"And what would you do," Mr. Stork asks,
"if there was a knife sticking out of his wound?"
"Freak out," says Laughing Boy loudly, from the floor.
I answer the question. "We'd leave it there," I say
while Gray-Haired Man gives me a reproachful glare.
"Correct," says Mr. Stork. "You could make things worse
by removing it yourself. Leave that for the paramedics."
He bobs his birdlike head on his birdlike neck.

"You all get an A on this one!" he announces merrily,
as though this was just a party game
and not someone's very life, dangling by a thread.

We high-five each other,
and the boy victim springs from the mat.
"Thanks, guys," he says. "You saved my life!"

Back home, I put my notes away in the desk.
Two more classes to go, and I will be certified
in triage. I sit at the square art table,
select a black pen, and sketch the long limbs
of our instructor onto thick white paper.

I hope
that I never have to help someone
who's been stabbed in the chest.
Still, if it happened? I could help.
I could make a difference.

And hopefully,
that difference
would be enough.

Lying

"Are you excited about your date on Saturday?"
Rachel asks. It's Thursday, and we're doing homework.
I roll onto my side, on Rachel's bed,
pushing books and papers aside.
"Yeah. And nervous."
"Did your mom give you a curfew?"
"Um, no." Come to think of it,
Mom barely responded
when I asked about going to the movies.

I don't tell Rachel about the dating site.
About the slick photos of men and women
all having the time of their lives.
About her mailbox being full.
"I'll see if she wants to go out tomorrow night.
We haven't done anything together in a while,"
I say.

So the next morning, I ask Mom,
half asleep over her coffee,
"Want to go out to dinner tonight?"
Her eyes widen; she sips too hard,
and in that microscopic window,
I know.
She has a date.
NEED A FOOT MASSAGE?
Oh, Lord. Surely she didn't pick him.

If not, then who? What? When?
Is he coming *here?*
"I have some plans tonight, actually,"
Mom says, busily mopping up
a microscopic speck of coffee.

I try to act nonchalant,
biting into my bagel. The bread
sticks in my mouth.
"Really?" My tone matches hers.
"What are you doing?"

"Going out with some friends."
Mom waves her hand dismissively.
"We'll probably get drinks or something.
Nothing exciting."

The ticking of the apple-shaped clock
fills the silence.
I chew, aware
that my mother
is lying.

Text Messages between Jane and Michael

J: You will not believe what Mom is doing.

M: Ballroom dancing lessons? Hot-air balloon classes?

J: She's DATING.

M: Seriously?

J: Yes.

M: What's he like?

J: I haven't met him. And there may be more than one. She's joined a dating site. And I think she's going out with someone tonight.

M: But you don't know that?

J: No, she said she's going out with friends.

M: Does she know you know about this dating site?

J: No. I kind of found it by accident.

M: I bet.

J: REALLY. Aren't you worried?

M: About you SPYING on people? Yes.

J: About MOM.

M: Mom is an adult. Leave her alone. Let her do this. It's about time, really.

J: She could go out with an ax murderer or something. She could get hurt.

M: She could find love. She could have a few laughs. She could see a movie and get free popcorn. Come on, Jane. Lighten UP. And DON'T tell her you found out about this dating thing. If she's not telling you, she's not ready.

J: SHE'S not ready? What about me?

M: This is not about you.

J: You are no help.

M: Thanks. :)

J: When are you coming home next?

M: Not for a few weeks. Have to hand in a film project. And finish a script.

J: My brother, the filmmaker.

M: We'll see.

J: Good luck.

M: Thanks!

J: CU.

Vuvuzela

I call Justin that evening
as I sit alone — alone because
my mother is out with someone,
I have no idea who, or where,
and she won't come clean.

Justin answers. Before I can say anything,
he blurts out, "I'm going to a *professional* soccer game!"
"That is fantastic!" I respond.
Justin is a big soccer fan. "When is it?"
"April. I can't *wait*. It's the L.A. Galaxy.
And Dad says he's going to get me
a *vuvuzela* for the game."
"A voozoo . . . what?"

He laughs, and happiness
spills from my heart to my toes.
There was a time when Justin
didn't laugh so freely.
There was a time when Justin
fell down in physical therapy,
getting used to his new leg,
and I wanted to destroy the world
and everyone in it to end his suffering.
I'm glad those days are behind us.

"A *vuvuzela* is a *horn*," he explains.
"They make this really loud honking sound.
Everyone brings them to big soccer matches."
"Well, I hope you have the loudest *vuvuzela* there."
"Do you have any new drawings for me?"
Justin asks, hopeful.
"I'll make you something,"
I promise. "Something really good."
Then I tell him to ask his parents
if they'll get us some more blue paint for our mural.

Justin runs off to ask. He returns, breathless.
"Dad says yes. We'll get some tomorrow.
He put it on the calendar."
I picture the busy calendar
they keep on their fridge, sprinkled
with Justin's action-packed schedule.
"Okay. See you next week, Justin."
"Will you have a drawing for me by then?" he asks.
Justin is nothing if not persistent.

"Yes. I will. I promise."
If Justin wants a drawing, he shall have one.
I want Justin to know
he can *always*
count on me.

Group Date

Finally. It's here.
Black turtleneck, a little makeup,
a lot of hair spray.
A small case of nerves.
Mom sends me off with a cheerful wave
and an annoying *My girl is growing up!*
vibe hanging all dewy in the air.

The movie is pretty good.
The pizza afterward is, too.
The kids are nice—
Matt, Jeremy, Will, Keisha, and Annie.
Even though it's all good, I want it to be over with.
What's wrong with me? I was excited—and now?
Now I want to go home.

Matthew is nice. Really nice.
But . . . the whole night is like
I'm auditioning for a part I don't even want
in some play I've never read.

Will, the one with a driver's license,
drives us all home after.
The first stop is my house.
"I had fun," Matthew says,
walking me to the door.

His hair is dark, feathery,
his eyes gray behind thin glasses.

"Me, too," I tell him,
wondering in a panic if he'll try to kiss me
right there on the front step.
"Thanks for inviting me."
"See you Monday," he says,
and with a small wave, he is gone.
I let myself in, relieved.
Thank goodness. No kiss.
But . . . maybe there was no kiss
because he figured out
he didn't want to kiss me any more than I
wanted to kiss him.
Maybe he'd sooner kiss a frog, Jane.

Either way, if I'm this relieved about a non-kiss,
then the next time Matthew asks me out —
if he asks me out —
I need to say
no.

For Justin

Coloring lightly,
then blending the pastels
with the tip of my little finger,
I carefully create Justin's drawing.
It's another picture of his dog, Spot —
Justin's favorite subject.
She's lying in the sun,
chewing on a ratty blue object
that Justin calls her sock.

The shadows are tricky,
and I find myself wanting to overdo them.
I fight off the urge, and soon
I have created something
that even I think
is beautiful.

I stare at it awhile, take a long break,
then come back and stare at it again.
Imperfections creep out at me,
but overall? This is *good*.
And there it is again, that rare, quiet flush
of satisfaction. This is like I used to do —
everything has come out as I intended.
And more important,
it is a gift I can give Justin

with complete happiness,
knowing he will like it.

I breathe a sigh of relief,
because this is not the outcome
of every piece of work I take on.

Oh — how I love this result,
this contentment, this process.
How I *miss* taking this kind of thing
for granted — just *expecting* it,
creating drawings all day long
without struggle, without frustration.

I pin the drawing to the wall.
Thank you for this moment, I think,
to whoever is listening.
For art. For color.

Thank you.

Order

After Justin has exclaimed with joy
over the portrait of Spot,
we get to work.
Tubs, jars, and gallons of paint
litter the floor of Justin's room.
With drop cloths spread everywhere,
and autumn sunshine drifting through the window,
Justin and I begin the electrifying process
of applying color to the white wall.

"I'm starting with this butterfly,"
Justin tells me, snatching up a purple pot of paint.
I hold out my hand. "No, no. That won't work."

He pauses, and I explain.
"See how small the butterfly is on that big bush?
The best thing to do is paint the bush first,
because it's larger. That way, you can fill in those large
areas of color quickly and allow yourself to bleed over a
little, into your butterfly shape, if needed.
You don't have to
be quite so careful in working around the butterfly,
like you would if it were already painted and perfect.
See what I mean?"

Justin cocks his head, studies the sketch on the wall,
then nods. "Yeah. I get it." He puts the purple paint down
and searches for the green. "Good idea."
We tackle our pieces of the mural, Justin with green
and me with a whole lot of blue for the sky.
I point out that it would also be a mistake
to paint the small birds flying in the sky,
then try to paint all that blue sky around them.
"I do the sky first, and everything else comes later,"
I say. Justin laughs. "What's so funny?" I ask.

He applies paint. "It feels like we're
creating a whole universe."
He grins up at me,
and I flush warm from my toes
to my head.
I love it when Justin is happy.

"I'm really glad we're doing this," he says.
"Me, too, Justin." I smile back at him. Then
I stretch my arm up high and rake a bold
swath of blue across the wall.
A sky is born.

4. Enter the School Art Competition

Each year our high school has a huge art contest.
Winners go on to compete
at a state level. Then a national level.
The first two years I entered,
I made it to state champion.
Once, I won first prize
for the entire western
United States.

Last year I was unable to enter
for obvious reasons.
Now I am ready to try again.
Granted, my art is still not the quality it was.
But it's coming back,
shred by shred, bit by bit.
After school every other Monday,
Mr. Musker works with me
on practice pieces. Today
we work on a pastel drawing of Justin.
"A little more depth here," Mr. M. says, pointing,
"and a little less white there.
That white is flattening out your surface."

I work, watching the colors take shape.
I put stock in Mr. Musker's words:
"Take heart in what progress you've made.
Always look ahead, not back."

I keep working, shading, blending,
ignoring the voice in my head that screams,
It's not perfect. Maybe it never will be.

This contest means a lot to me.
I can't put into words exactly
what it means to me,
because I'm not entirely sure.
Proof that I didn't lose my ability entirely?
Evidence that I haven't shriveled up
and fallen off the art planet,
that I do still, in fact, create,
and that my creations have merit?
Or is it strictly an ego thing?

I don't know.
But I'm not letting another year,
my *final* year to enter,
slip by
without
trying.

Letter from Andrea
Culver City, California

Dear Jane,

I recently read your follow-up story in a magazine. I have to say, I've been wondering about you and was so glad to see the story, though I would have liked to have heard some direct quotes from you. The story made it sound like you're fully recovered and back in school. I hope that's true and that your life is back to normal and you are well.

I lost a dear friend to cancer right about the time you had your accident. I remember watching your story on the news, and seeing how young you were, and thinking about my friend, who was young also. I've spent a lot of time wondering why life isn't fair. It isn't, is it?

You really are an inspiration, and I just wanted to write and tell you that. You inspire me to avoid feeling sorry for myself. You inspire me to be grateful for my health and for all that I have. The article mentioned that you volunteer at the hospital and that you intend to be a nurse. Incredible! You inspire me to help others. Truly. I signed up and have gone through training so that I, too, can help out at my local hospital. It's something my friend — the one I lost to cancer — always encouraged me to do, but I never got around to it. Well, now I have. Thank you so much for being such a role model of bravery, compassion, and courage. I wish you the best.

Your friend,

Andrea

Responsibility

Okay. I am not new
to letters from strangers,
but this latest surge is getting to me.
The first few months after my accident,
I was nearly drowned in the rivers
of mail and cards that came my way —
many of them suggesting that my accident
was no accident but part of some divine plan,
that I had a purpose yet to carry out.

The letters trickled off in time.
Now, with that one little article,
here they come again. And like last time,
many of them suggest that I have a role to play,
an obligation I must figure out,
and thanks to misquoting
what I said, a lot of people assume that
obligation is the heroic
and selfless act of becoming a nurse.

Why didn't I make it more clear
that I was undecided? Why didn't I
stress that art was in the running, too?
Why did I even answer her at all?
See? This only reinforces my theory:
being a hermit is good for your health.

And silence
is truly golden.

I'm touched that people care enough
to write.
But honestly? Their care,
their letters — they boil down to one thing:
pressure.

Deciding what to do with my future
is hard enough.
Feeling the weight of so many opinions
crush the scale in favor of one thing
over another?

It makes the decision
even harder.

Matthew

Leaving class, Matthew stops me.
"You want to go to the movies again?
Just us this time?"
He bites his lip nervously,
fidgets with the zipper on his jacket.
He looks vulnerable, and suddenly
I think how I'd feel if I were in his shoes,
doing the asking. Putting my courage out there.

"Yes," I answer. "That would be . . . fun."
Matthew grows a fraction taller.
"Great. Saturday night?
I'll call you and we'll pick what to see."
Then we head our separate ways,
him going right, me going left.

I said I'd say no next time.
And I caved. Don't cave, Jane.

How can I not cave? Did you see his face?

Well, either way, I'm going.
But unless my feelings change,
this date needs to be our last.

Baking

The next afternoon, my friends gather
at my house. After mugs of hot chocolate,
we get to work.
We're baking Halloween cupcakes
and decorating them using my newest fancy tools.
"You sure have gotten into the cake thing,"
Angie says, examining a rosette tip.

"Yeah, and you're really *good* at it."
Trina points to the remaining portion
of the cake I made two days ago,
decorated in roses and leaves.
"Would you be willing to make
the cake for my birthday party? *Please?*"
"Of course I will, silly," I tell her.
"I'll make you a three-tiered princess cake."
"Great!" Trina says. "Whatever that is."

Elizabeth arranges her pile of purple-frosted cupcakes.
"How did you learn all this?"
"Reading lots of books, and watching
videos on the Internet." I pass her a towel,
and she mops up a cascade of spilled sprinkles.
"You should open a shop," Trina says.
"She can't do that. She's going to be busy
with Jane's Art Gallery," Elizabeth says.

Angie shakes her head.
"Jane is going to be a nurse."
"Guys," I say, "I haven't decided."

"I better not eat any more," Trina says.
"I don't want to outgrow my prom gown."
We stare. "You have your gown already?"
I ask. "Prom isn't till spring!"
Next thing you know, that's all we can talk about: *prom*.

"Can't wait to see Scott in a tux,"
Angie sighs dreamily. "Who are you taking, Trina?"
"Kevin. What about you, Elizabeth?"
Elizabeth shakes her head. "I don't know.
I don't care who it is, as long as he buys me a limo."
Rachel licks icing from a spoon.
"I don't need a limo.
Just someone really special."
"Like *Tom Mayfield*?" Angie teases,
and when Rachel's jaw drops,
we crow with laughter.
"Is it *that* obvious?" Rachel asks.

We tease, we joke, we bake, and
before long, our decorated cupcakes
are lined up on pretty plates.

I snap a photo,
my friends and their cupcakes,
a moment frozen in time
when we are all still just "us,"
with no great distance

or great decisions

cutting us apart.

Sent

The little white arrow hovers
on the computer screen.
My palm is damp over the mouse.

"Just send it already!" Michael gripes.
He snatches the mouse, hits SEND,
and just like that, my first college application
is sent. "Was that so bad?" he says.
"You have *four* applications ready.
Just send them.
Besides, I need the computer."

I try to think of something snarky to say
about his total lack of ceremony.
This is a big moment, after all. This is the moment
when hope is still alive and options feel bountiful.

But I'm with him. With three more clicks of the mouse,
the applications blink away to their destinations.
Two nursing schools, two art schools. Two local,
two far away. I can expect to hear back
in March. Right around my birthday.
Let's hope it's good news.

Rain Date

The movie theater
is downright cavernous
without the extra bodies
of a social group.
Tonight it's just Matthew and me.
We chat, we eat, we watch the previews,
and Matthew jokes about them in such witty ways.

But the whole time,
I am so stiff. So wooden. So remote.
My entire body seems made from concrete.
Matthew is so funny.
But he is a stranger to me,
out of context outside the science lab,
and what's more, I keep thinking
I'm in somebody else's seat.
Or maybe Matthew is the one
in the wrong chair.

Choking with guilt
makes it hard to eat popcorn,
so I quit, and quietly, thankfully,
we fall silent once the movie starts.
I have no business being here.
Why did I even come? I thought . . .
Well, what *did* I think?

That Matthew might grow on me?
Like a fungus or something?
Is that what I think of him?
I need to get brave and end this.
But how do you break up with someone
you're barely dating?

Later his mom picks us up.
She drives us home in the pelting rain.
"How was the movie?" she asks.
"Funny," Matthew says.
"Really good," I add.
His fingers wrap around mine
in the chilly backseat.

On the porch,
his mom parked a discreet distance away,
Matthew and I have a nanosecond alone.
"I had a great time," Matthew says.
"Me, too, and thank you for taking me."
I stare down at my shoes,
listening to the splatter of rain falling,
about to muster the courage
to walk into the house,
close the door,
and next time he calls, explain

and say *"I don't really like you that way,
Matthew. I'm sorry."*

But when I look up,
Matthew's face is startlingly close.
"Good night," he says,
and before I can even blink,
his lips meet mine.

He kisses me.
Time stands still.
Cold rain spatters on our heads.
Then he hovers a moment.
"Bye, Jane," he says, his breath warm on my face.
He takes two steps backward
before turning and melting away
into the wet darkness.

First

Soft and warm.
That's what his kiss was.
Soft
and
warm.

Mark it off the bucket list.
Shouldn't I be happy?
My first kiss.
My first
one
ever.

But . . . kissing Matthew was like . . .
kissing a pillow, or a relative's cheek,
or something not quite real.

Still — however it felt?
It was, undeniably,

my
first
kiss.

Art Lesson

The paintbrushes lie on a ladder rung;
the paint sits untouched.
Today's mural-painting session
has been derailed for a while,
all because Justin made one remark.
Wistfully, he said, "I wish I could draw."

Well. You can bet I don't let a remark
like that go unanswered. And not with a
Oh, I'm sure you can draw beautifully
pat on the head, either. Justin deserves
more than that. Justin deserves an art lesson.

"Her nose doesn't look right," he tells me
from where we are spread out on the floor,
paper before us, pencils in hand. Spot models
obligingly, lolling in a window-square of sunlight.
"And her eyes are weird. See? I told you."
I look over his shoulder. "You skipped
an important step. Before you place the eyes and nose
on her head, you have to divide that head into quadrants.
Like this." On my own paper, I make an oval
for Spot's head. Then I run the pencil back and forth,
finding the curving, dividing lines that separate
Spot's face. One is vertical, one is horizontal.
Now her head shape is divided into fourths.

"Show me where those lines intersect," I say.

Justin puts his finger on the spot. "Good," I tell him.

"That is the exact center of Spot's face.
When you start to add details to it, like her eyes,
you can attach them to the places
they are supposed to be,
because now you have a framework to guide you.
Her features won't be randomly floating on her face.
For instance, her muzzle would be centered there,
wouldn't it?" I sketch a little rectangle.

Justin picks up his pencil and does the same, carefully.

"And her nose goes . . . ?" I ask.

Justin puts a black blob on the end of the muzzle.

He cocks his head. "That looks pretty good!"

He glances at mine. "But not as good as yours."

I nudge him. "Don't compare your work to others'.
You'll always find someone who you think is better
than you. If you get wrapped up in that,
you'll never create anything."

He sighs, examines his blocked-in head shapes, and then
places two dots on the horizontal line, on either side
of the muzzle. "That's where her eyes go. Right?"
I wait for him to answer his question, and he does.

"That looks better!" He colors in the eyes

boldly, bringing Spot to life right there on that paper.
"That actually looks like her!"

"Of course it does, silly," I tell him. Together,
we continue sketching, placing body parts, smoothing
out a paw here, a tail there. I show Justin how to make
a vanishing point on his paper for reference, and how
all lines flow toward that point, giving his drawing
dimension.
"That is so cool," he says, eyes wide. His brow furrows
as he works. "Thanks for showing me this."

I don't know how much time trickles away
while we lie on our stomachs, drawing and coloring
and drawing some more. And I don't care.
Because an afternoon like this, with a good friend
and fellow artist, can't be measured in hours.
It can only be received with quiet gratitude,
which it is.

Thanksgiving

It's just the three of us this year,
Mom and Michael and me.
With Mom dating,
will this be our last year like this?

The table is laden with a banquet,
and we savor every bite.
There is a groan when I bring out the desserts.
Pecan pie and a two-tiered cake
decorated in basket-weave icing.
"Jane, that is a gorgeous cake," Mom says.

After dessert, none of us moves to clean up.
We are too full. Later we'll watch football on TV.
I have a new book to read.
Mom will pick up her knitting.
Michael will make a fire in the fireplace,
and Mabel will stretch out in front of it.
At some point, we'll all fall asleep.

There are some things
you like being able to count on.
Traditions like this
are one of them.

Triage, Class Two

"Today we will talk about prioritizing."
Mr. Stork projects images onto the screen.
"When you are called on to help
in an emergency," he says, "the reality is
that not every person is in the exact same level
of emergency. Some people need to be seen
immediately. Some people can wait a little,
to make room for those who can't.
And, frankly, some people can't be saved.
Or they may be dead." He holds up a black tag.
"That is what this is for." He proceeds
to talk about the other colored tags.
They each stand for something. *Minor.*
Significant. Immediate. Deceased.

"In triage, you determine which tag
to put on everyone," he says.
"It will help medical staff know
where to start when they arrive."
After lecturing a bit longer, he once again
asks us to form groups of four.

In silent agreement, our same little group
gravitates together, a ragged band of sheep
facing a wolf. Sweater Lady is wearing a dress today.
Laughing Boy grins.
"I don't have to be on the floor this time. Cool."

Mr. Stork deposits a swath of tags
in my hand. He gives Sweater Lady
a sheet of paper. "Here is your injury. Everyone?
Decide what tag to put on her."

He moves off as Sweater Lady reads,
"Burns on legs and arms. Facial contusions.
Possible head injury." She puts the paper down
abruptly. "Can I just sit in a chair for this?
I really don't want to lie on the floor."

We all murmur agreement, muttering
over the sheet of paper.
"First thing we do is evaluate her," I say.
Gray-Haired Man says, "I know."
"We should start with skin color, temperature,
pulse," I say, consulting my notes.
Gray-Haired Man says, "I *know*."
He glares fiercely at his notepad.
Laughing Boy snaps his fingers. "Ooh, ooh.
Head injury. We need to see if she has a concussion."

"We ask her questions," Gray-Haired Man says quickly.
"Test her mental alertness." He turns to the woman.
"What is your name? What day is it?
Who's the president?"
"Who's the *president*?" the woman repeats, flustered.

I flap my hand. "You don't have to answer.
We just write down that we assessed your memory."

We scribble.
"Now we assess her burns," Gray-Haired Man says.
We do. We assess the contusions, too.
Then we decide how to label her.
In the end, we reach a unanimous decision.
Significant.
"Cool," says the boy. "I like that tag."

I touch the tag. *Significant.*
It does have a tone of insistence.
Of demand.
Of declaration.
Aren't we all significant, after all?
It was significant that I encountered a shark,
nearly died, and lost my arm. Why did that happen?
And I'm not *deceased.* I survived.
Luck? Or a reason?
The need to figure that out
seems *immediate.*

We place the tag in Sweater Lady's lap.
And I wonder,
what would it be like if we all wore tags
declaring the state of our injuries?
Because we all have them — call them
what you will. We all walk around

with thorns on our shoulders,
in our heads, our hearts, our past,
our present.
Significant. Minor. Immediate.

A tag would speed things up, wouldn't it?
And maybe even help
everyone know
just how kind they need to be.
Every day.

Significant

The class concludes with everyone
sharing their results. "I was beyond saving,"
a woman says in disgust.
"My arms were severed."

In the silence, I am aware of the pull
of every pair of eyes in the room,
straining not to look at me
and my severed arm.

At home I put away my notes
and slide into bed.
Red, that's what my tag would have been
in that moment, when the lady
mentioned severed arms.
Red cheeks, on every face in the room.

Immediate
would have been the classification.
Immediate
is the need
to tell everyone,
"It's okay, really. Let's just move on.
No need to be embarrassed.
I've seen and heard it all before."

And the other thing?
Tonight, when Mom brought me home,
I walked into the kitchen
and saw two plates
still on the table, covered in crumbs,
and two wineglasses.
I pretended not to notice
when she quickly snatched them up
and clattered them into the sink.
Someone shared dinner
at home
with my mother
while I was gone.

Label that one
SIGNIFICANT.

Osmosis

"Another D in science,"
I tell Rachel as I slide into a seat
next to her at lunch.

"But we studied so hard together,"
Rachel says. "You *had* that one."

"I thought so, too."
Trina and Elizabeth and Angie join us,
their trays laden with pizza.
"What's wrong?" Angie asks.
I sigh. "I am failing science."
"I got a C in social studies," Angie counters.
"You've *always* been bad at science," Trina adds.
"Yes. But now my grades matter. For college.
It's something you really need for nursing programs —
good grades in science."

They all start eating. Not me. I'm too worried.
"You know what I need?" I say. "Osmosis.
I need to find someone smart at science
and sit next to them. Then their knowledge
will ooze into my brain by proximity."

Rachel says, "Don't ask me.
I am barely getting by in that class."
Elizabeth snaps her fingers. "A tutor.

That's what you need.
My brother is great at science.
I'll check with him."

Of *course.*
It's like a switch flips on in my head,
shedding God's first light on a gaping canyon.
"That's a great idea.
Check with him, and thanks!"

A tutor. Maybe that's the key.
Someone to translate
all those periodic table numbers
and signs and facts
into plain English for me.
Why didn't I think of it before now?

Beneath the lunch table,
I cross my fingers,
hoping that this is just the thing
I need.

Mom, Knitting

That night, as another flare-up
of burning arm pain finally ebbs away,
Elizabeth calls.
"I asked my brother
about tutoring you. He can't.
He got a job after school and doesn't have time."
I sigh as Mabel nudges me with her wet nose.
"That's okay. Thanks for checking."

"He said to try the community college," Elizabeth adds.
"Go to the cafeteria or the main office.
Kids put signs up on the bulletin boards there.
There's usually someone advertising tutoring."
"Okay, I'll check it out. And thanks!"
I hang up and give Mabel a kiss.
"Who was that?" Mom asks.
I tell her about Elizabeth's idea
of a tutor.

Mom listens. She doesn't say,
"You have always been bad in science"
or *"What matters is that you try your very best."*
She just picks up her knitting bag.
"Tutoring is a great idea. Why didn't I think of it?
If you can't find anyone at Sequoyah, I'll check at my school."

I realize I never asked if she'd mind paying
for this imaginary tutor. Now I don't have to.
She's already said yes.
And that's one of the great things about Mom.
I watch her sink into the couch
and flip on the TV, pulling out a ball of yellow yarn
and heavy knitting needles.

I think of
NEED A FOOT MASSAGE?
and a wave of something—
pity . . . anger? —
passes through me.
I think about her mystery dinner date,
her supposed nights "working late,"
and I hope that the person she was with
made her laugh and treated her right.

All these years my dad has been gone.
Mom's a good person.
She deserves someone
who's not a creep.
She deserves to be loved.

Letter from Paula
Burbank, California

Dear Jane,

I remember hearing about your story last year, and I've always wondered how you are. I was so relieved to see the follow-up article on you. Good for you for getting back to school and moving on. I have talked about you with my students, both last year and this year. I am an elementary-school teacher and often talk to my students about people with disabilities, and how we view them, and how we can so easily be insensitive to them. We talk about how we'd feel if we were in another person's shoes — a person like you.

It is a testament to your courage that you continue to live a normal life and be a role model to everyone with your determination. I hope you continue to heal and that you have no bad memories of that day. I hope you look forward, and not back.

If you are ever willing, it would be remarkable to have you come talk to the kids at my school. I think you'd make an incredible impression, and drive home what we talk about when we discuss people with differences, and how really, we are all just alike. I will enclose my contact information — please think about it.

Best wishes,

Paula

One Second

I'm buying a soda from the vending machine
in the hospital hallway when suddenly
sirens go off and someone on the intercom
cries, "Code blue! Third floor, code blue!"

In a flash, a barrage of people in scrubs
rush past. I don't even know where they came from.
Someone crashes into me and sends me smack
into the vending machine. My soda can falls to the floor,
goes spinning wildly among scrambling shoes,
and my elbow throbs crazily from where it got hit.

They're gone and I pick up the can.
Code blue is serious, in case you didn't know.
Code blue means someone has gone into cardiac arrest.
Someone is dying right now,
and everyone is doing everything they can to prevent that.

I think I saw Lindsey in the midst of the chaos.
I picture myself as part of that group someday,
a person running to stop death from claiming another.
Once inside that hospital room, what would I see?
What would I do? Rip off someone's hospital gown,
apply electric paddles? Stand by with shots of Adrenalin?
Would my training get through the shock
of seeing someone already blue-lipped and staring?
I shudder. I know this is part of nursing.

It's not all hand holding and coloring books
and people getting well.
Sometimes my patients would die.

Later, Lindsey sags at her desk, draining a cup of coffee.
"I'm sorry," I tell her, even though I didn't know the patient,
an elderly man who had only checked in last night.
She throws the cup in the trash can. "Thank you, honey.
I tell you. This is a part of the job you never get used to."
She dabs at her eyes. "I am constantly amazed
how things can change in a second. Just one *second*."
She sniffs and throws the tissue away.
"That man was *so* nice. He was here for minor surgery.
Then he had a heart attack. We couldn't save him."

You'd think a hospital would be the one place
you could survive having a heart attack.
But I guess sometimes you just can't save a person.
Sometimes it's too late.

The rest of the day,
I think about that poor man, his family, his life.
And I think about the words *too late*.
If I became a nurse and had regrets
what would I tell myself? *"Too late, Jane. Sorry."*

If I become an artist, I will regret turning away
from my reason
for wanting to nurse in the first place:

to help other people.
If I become a nurse, I will regret closing the door
on art, a heartbeat that has been part of me
my whole life.
Either way you slice it, I sense regret waiting for me
at the end of all this. How did I end up in this position?
At one time, my life was so simple.
It was so *clear.*

I'd give anything to have that clarity back,
even if it were
for just
one second.

Text Messages between Jane and Mom

M: Will be home late 2nite. Will you be OK?

J: Yes. Trina coming over 4 dinner & homework. What R U doing?

M: I have to work late.

J: Oh?

M: Yes. Call me if you need me. Love U. C U about 10.

J: OK.

Triage, Class Three

It is our final triage class. After taking notes
and watching a grim slide show,
we are ready for practice.
"A bomb just went off," Mr. Stork says theatrically.
"You have been asked to help with the wounded.
Form groups of four and begin."

Silently, our group clusters together again,
me, Laughing Boy, Sweater Lady, and Gray-Haired Man,
an assortment of oddly matched people
who, apparently, have a need to know
how to deal with torn arteries,
scorched limbs, and ruptured lives.
Mr. Stork taps Gray-Haired Man.
"You're it," he says, handing him a note.

"Massive bleeding from the leg,"
Gray-Haired Man reads. "Burns on legs and arms."
He sighs, lowers himself to the mat,
and removes his glasses. "Ready."
We snatch up the survival kit.
"Massive bleeding from the leg could mean
a ruptured artery," Sweater Lady says. "What do we do?"

"Clamp it," I say, and we find a clamp.
Laughing Boy takes the clamp. "I'll do it."
I remind Sweater Lady that we need to assess his vitals.

We take his pulse and listen to his breathing.
We check his pupil dilation with a small flashlight,
and then record his skin color and temperature.
"Now what?" Laughing Boy says,
rummaging through our kit.
"Clean the wounds," I say, "and bind the leg."

"I think that's it," Sweater Lady says.
Mr. Stork swoops in. "All done? Let me see your notes."
I hand them over; he nods while reading them.
"Very good. But you overlooked one small thing."
Gray-Haired Man's eyes fly open.
"What?" he demands. "What could they
have *possibly* forgotten? They did *everything* to me."
Mr. Stork blinks. "They did not reassess
your circulation. That is critical.
The clamp could be put on too tightly.
You have to follow up continuously when using a clamp."

Defeat settles over us in a damp cloud.
Gray-Haired Man stands and puts his glasses back on.
"It's okay," he says. He claps Laughing Boy on the shoulder.
"Come on, guys. Shake it off."
He sounds for all the world like a coach of some kind,
and I wonder suddenly about all of them.
Who are they?

"By the way," Gray-Haired Man says, as though
reading my mind. "I'm Martin.

And I think you three might just be
as competitive as I am. Nice to meet you."
We all shake hands then, smiling a little
at our late introductions. "I'm Penny,"
Sweater Lady says.
"And I'm Josh," the boy says.
He looks familiar, sort of.
"Jane," I say,
and we all nod at one another once more.

"One mistake is not bad," Martin says.
"We've earned our certificate.
We should be happy about that."
He's right. Still. You can't *forget* things
when a person's life is on the line.
You just can't.

Mr. Stork tells the class that we all passed,
that we are one of the sharpest classes
he's ever taught. "Good luck," he tells us.
"Nice meeting you. And let's hope
you never need this training."

I tape the triage certificate to the wall,
next to the CPR one.
Check this off the bucket list.
Clean or sloppy, good or bad,
I did it.
I really did it.

Review

Bucket List for Senior Year

1. Apply to nursing school and art college.
2. Choose one or the other.
3. Become fully certified in CPR, first aid, and triage.
4. Enter the school art competition.
5. Win the school art competition.
6. Qualify for and enter the West Coast Wings art competition.
7. Win the West Coast Wings art competition.
8. Go to prom.
9. Bake a wedding cake.
10. Save a life.

I can check off number one.
I can check off number three.
And I sure am working
on perfecting my cake-making skills.

Everything else?
Everything else remains to be done.

Party Time

After math, Trina pries herself
out of Kevin's arms long enough
to snag me in the hallway.
She hands me a folded up piece of pink paper.
"You already know, but here's an invitation."

I shake open the paper. "A week from Friday?"
I pretend to think hard, then sigh heavily.
"I *guess* I can make it . . . I suppose.
Maybe I'll even bring a cake."

She slugs me on the shoulder.
"Jane, I can't wait to see the cake."
Then she adds, "Matthew is coming.
So you guys can go together
or just meet up there, either one."
"I hope you didn't invite him
just for me," I say, horrified.
Trina rolls her eyes. "No, it's not about *you*.
He's good friends with Kevin."
I look at Kevin, busy burying his nose
in Trina's neck. He and Matthew?
Studious Matthew?
Well. Just goes to show, people are surprising.

"I'll be there, and the cake, too," I tell her.
I leave them snuzzling each other's necks

like drug-sniffing dogs.
What's it like to feel that way toward someone?
So passionate? So happy?
What's it like to not even care
that people stare while you kiss?

Sometimes I think
I may never know.

Letter from Rianna
Glendale, California

Dear Jane,

My name is Rianna, and I am in tenth grade. I am writing to ask you if you would consider letting me interview you and write an article about you for my school magazine. I think your story is amazing and that a lot of people would like to hear more about you.

It would be a huge help to me to have a story like yours for our magazine. I love being a reporter and can't think of anyone I would like to interview more. Please contact me at my e-mail address if you are willing to do this for me.

Thanks!
Rianna

Fingers

Bucket list item #2:
Choose nursing school or art school.

I put the list back in the drawer.
I can't sit around agonizing forever.
And I can't keep stalling, either.
If I choose nursing,
I will *have* to have good grades
in science. So this afternoon,
I put aside the etching
I'm working on and
ride my bike to the local college.

The cafeteria
is filled to the rafters
with the smell of onions, grease,
and murky mop water.
The buzz of the crowd fills my ears.
I stand there a minute, not sure where to go.
On the brick wall, I spy a bulletin board
exploding with papers
pointing every which way.
Some are pinned on top of others.
Some are pink and some are green.
I walk over and investigate.

There's a car for sale, a lost necklace,
and lots of ads seeking roommates to share rent.
There is one note advertising tutoring.
For *math*.

Well! I guess I imagined I'd walk in here,
and all my problems would be solved.
I guess I figured I'd just snap my fingers
and get what I wanted.
I guess I thought
I was someone else in some other world—
a TV show, perhaps.
I guess I was stupid.

However—maybe the math tutor
knows someone who, with a little coaxing,
will be my science tutor.
As I reach for the tab at the bottom of the sign—
those little half-cut-up tabs
you can tear off and take home
with the phone number written on it—
my fingers bump into another set of fingers,
slender fingers,
reaching for the same thing
at the same time.

I look up.
And nearly fall over.

"Sorry," he says. "Wait . . . Jane?"
That voice,
deep and husky,
that dimple in his chin.
I am staring into the face

of Max Shannon.

Burgers and Salad

"I almost didn't recognize you,"
Max says, all dark and handsome and damp curls.
"Your hair got so long."

"Hi, Max."
I want to say something friendly or funny,
but all I can think of is how his eyes sparkle
and his smile
is like an answer to a question.
So I ask, "Do you go to school here?"

Oh, Lord, Jane. So mundane.
He nods, and I can't tell
what he's thinking,
but he's thinking something.
Something serious.
"Yeah. I go here. Hey,
can I buy you a burger?
I was just coming in for lunch."

Lunch? Seriously? Does he think he's obligated?
Is this sympathy for me, the person needing a tutor?
Wait . . . He was reaching for the number, too.
So maybe he needs a tutor.
How could I say no, anyway? And why would I?
Should I?

He cocks his head and smiles.
"I forgot how you like to think things through
before you answer a question."
I laugh, heat flooding my face. "Yep."
"I like that about you," he adds,
and I think maybe he means it.
I summon a deep breath.
"I'd love to have a burger."
I make my face very grave.
"But . . . I can't."
He raises an eyebrow.
Do I dare hope that he looks disappointed?

"Because . . . I'm a vegetarian," I explain.
He pretends to be horrified.
"Oh, no. You're one of *them*."
"Yeah."
"So, no burger. I'll buy you a *salad*. Okay?"

Don't grin like that, Jane.
You look like a predator
about to lunge at his face.

"A salad sounds perfect."

All Through Lunch

I can barely focus on what he's saying
or what I'm saying
because that shooting pain in my stump,
the pain that comes and goes at will,
has decided to come.
In full, demanding presence.

Stabbing, throbbing, pillaging,
and burning. It's all I can do
not to take off my prosthesis
and claw at the spot that
hurts.

I hate it.

Hate it

hate it

hate it.

Phone Number

The pain dies down.
Max walks me to the bike rack.
"So you need a tutor in science, huh?"
he asks, resuming our conversation.

"Yes, I do," I answer.
Max sees me reaching for my bike,
and he grabs it for me,
yanks it out of its spot, and holds it
while I slide my purse into the basket.

"That's right. You're interested in medicine, aren't you?
Physical therapy or nursing?" he asks.
I bend my head to my purse. *He remembers.* "Yes."
Something buzzes, and he uses one hand
to pull his phone from his sweatshirt pocket.
"Mind if I answer this? It'll be quick."

I give him a nod, like a queen or something,
and busy myself with my purse
while he speaks into the phone.
"Hi, Sarah. Yes. I got the number you wanted.
Ready?"

I am suddenly very busy with my jacket zipper.
Sarah.
A girlfriend, no doubt.

What am I doing? Why do I kid myself?
Max is being kind — that's all there is to this.
"His name is Rick and it just says 'math tutor,'"
Max says into the phone.
Then he reads Sarah the number from the tab
he pulled off the bulletin board.

Of course. Max does not need a math tutor for himself.
Max doesn't need anything.
He's just fine the way he is.
Unlike me — needy, ignorant Jane.

Max snaps the phone shut.
"Sorry about that. I told her I'd get the number for her."
I force a smile. "No problem."
I need to leave before things get worse,
but Max is still holding the handlebars of my bike.
"How about me?" he says. "Would you consider that?"
I blink a couple of times. "Uh . . . for what?"

"Tutoring. I got A's all last year in science.
You have Mr. Veckio, right? That's who I had."

Seriously?
"Oh. Are you sure?"
I must be doing a good acting job,
because my voice sounds normal.

Max says, "Yeah. It's a great idea.
I could use the money, and I can help you out."

Well. This day has taken a turn
I never would have imagined.

What about Sarah?
What *about* her?
She may be his girlfriend.
And she may *not* be.
Besides, this is not engaging in infidelity.
This is not a marriage proposal.
This is science tutoring.
With *Max.*

"When can we start?" I ask.
He considers. "A week from Tuesday? About seven?"
"Great."
"I'll come to your house."
"Okay."
"I remember where it is."
"Good."

He suggests a price for his time.
I tell him I'll check with Mom.
My whole body is heating up;
I can't believe we're making plans to meet.
He asks for my phone number,
and I try not to stutter when I give it to him.

"See you next Tuesday," he says.
Then we part ways, Max returning to his world,
me returning to mine,
my heart thudding, my palm sweating.
Max is coming to my house. *Mine.*

As I pedal,
wind blowing through my hair,
I think that
at this moment

I   could   fly

all the way

home.

Last Year

Max, the senior, the swim-team captain,
the only guy who did not stare
at me that first day back to school,
gave me a ride home
from school
three different times.

We laughed and talked
each time,
and each time
I found out something new about him.

First ride:
He likes *White Fang* better than
Call of the Wild.
He's a reader, like me.

Second ride:
He started swimming when he was five.
He had asthma.
His mom got advice somewhere
that swimming would help his asthma get better.
It didn't.
But he fell in love
with swimming, and now
he could never give it up. Ever.

Third ride:
His old brown car coughed and sputtered
and nearly died
three blocks from my house.
He brought it back to life
by pumping the gas pedal
and flipping the ignition off and on.
When I joked,
"Maybe it's time for a new car,"
he told me that the car
had belonged to his mother,
who died two years earlier of cancer,
and even though the car has seen better days,
Max won't let it go.
"It would be like letting *her* go," he said.
"Does that sound weird?"

"Of course not," I told him.
I longed, at that moment,
to tell him that my dad died of cancer, too,
and that I have a coat of his
I keep in my closet,
and sometimes I breathe deeply into it,
trying to smell the aftershave
of a man I don't remember.

"I still miss her sometimes, you know?"
Max said. Then he shrugged
and fiddled with the radio.

I wanted to ask Max
to tell me more about his mom,
to brush the curl off his forehead,
and even though it was like wishing for a star,
I longed to kiss him,
just once.

Most of all,
I longed to have both arms again,
for just a moment,
so I could wrap him
in a hug.

Text Messages between Jane and Mom

J: That pain came back today. Please make dr app for me asap.

M: I'm sorry that happened. Already made appt for Wed at 4.
R U OK now?

J: Yes.

M: Need me to come home?

J: No. I'm fine.

M: OK. In class now. Need to run. Text if U need me. Love you.

J: Love U 2.

What on Earth

Rachel calls, says,
"Did you go to the college
and look for a tutor?"

And just like that, I hear myself say,
"No. Not yet."

"Oh. Well, I hope you find someone,"
Rachel says. She yawns.
"Gotta go. Have to finish up homework."

"Okay, see you."
I hang up, walk into the kitchen,
and pull out ingredients to make brownies.
I'm even humming.
A girl who just lied to her best friend,
baking and humming.

What on earth am I doing?
I don't understand why I just lied to Rachel.
Or why I'm acting like I didn't.

Still. Here I am,
lying to my best friend.
Here I am,
baking brownies,
and humming.

Equation

1 Brownie + 1 Lie to Best Friend

÷

3 Brownies + 2 Hours Spent on New Painting

÷

1 *Ugly Painting* that Ends Up in the TRASH

×

1 More Brownie + 1 Cup of Coffee at Midnight

———————————————————————

1 Long

Sleepless Night

Neuroma

"This is what's happening:
the nerve endings at the end of your arm
have bundled up and grown into a snarl,"
Dr. Kim explains, examining the X-rays.
He adds that the snarl
is rubbing against my prosthetic arm
and generally wiggling itself
into a ball of tight, sharp agony.
"How often does this flare up, Jane?" he asks.

"Uh . . . a few times a week?" I say.
Why do I sound like I'm asking *him* a question?

He kneads my stump with gentle fingers.
"Mm-hmm. When it does flare up,
how would you rate the pain,
on a scale of one to ten?"
"I'd say it's about an eight point three."

Dr. Kim says, "That is very specific.
I am sorry to hear this. I had hoped
to avoid this, but with amputation,
it is always a possibility."

"What can we do about it?" I ask,
wincing as he probes a tender spot.
Dr. Kim lets go of my arm and returns to the folder

of papers on the table.
It's very thick.
He begins writing on the top sheet of paper.

"First thing we'll do is have you stop
wearing your prosthesis. I want you to go
two weeks without it.
Then we'll send you in for a fitting adjustment.
Sometimes that's enough to avoid further flare-ups.
Also, we'll try some non-invasive treatments.
Sometimes those help."

I don't like this—
that's two *sometimes*es
and no *definites*.
"And if those *don't* work?" I ask.
Then we'll do a neurectomy," he says.
"A what?" I ask.

Dr. Kim adjusts his glasses.
"A surgical procedure
where we sever the snarled nerve endings,
then fold and tuck the ends
into a better location,
under fat or muscle tissue.
We move them away from the end of your arm
the best we can."

Mom asks him something else,
but all I can hear is the roar in my ears.
Surgery.
Again.

Here. In this hospital.
Again.

In a stiff bed, with arm pain,
ugly black stitches,
pain pills and bleary head
and dry mouth
and recovery struggles
and misery.

Again.

Have Faith

"Jane?" Dr. Kim bends slightly toward me.
"Are you all right?"
I nod. Then I start to cry.
What the heck?
I thought I was a pillar of strength by now.
Mom puts her arm around me.
"Honey, don't worry."

"It wouldn't be like last time,"
Dr. Kim says. He holds out a tissue,
and I take it. "A neurectomy
is not major surgery.
One or two nights in the hospital.
You'd be back in business in a week or two.
And you'll feel better once we take care of this."
He returns to his notes.
"I'm scheduling the ultrasound therapy,
and I'm going to give you several treatments
you can do at home when the pain flares up.
If by some chance these methods
are enough to ease the situation, then surgery
won't be necessary.
You never know."

He gives me a forced smile.
Looking at his hands, I can already see
the knife in them.

"It's going to be all right," he says.
Easy for him to say.
Why do people *say* things like that?
Because it's true, or they *want* it to be true?
The reality of this moment?
Nobody knows *anything*
for sure.

Mom says, "Have faith, honey."

I try to have faith.
But riding home,
the pain flares up again,
wickedly,
and it's all I can do
to just

breathe.

What If?

How dumb was I to think that my journey would end
at a defined time, anyway? Everyone *told* me
this was a situation I'd be dealing with for *life*.

What if
Dr. Kim slips while doing the surgery,
severing something critical, and makes things worse?
What if
I turn out to be one of the rare people
who die from non-major surgery
or end up worse than before?
What if
they cut this lump out and another one grows in its
place?
What if
I have to have surgeries my whole life?
What if
by the time they get done,
there's nothing left of me?

What if?

Practice

Our skies have been formed.
Our clouds have been dotted
and feathered into convincing
shapes, drifting in the blue.
Our fields and flowers are through,
and now comes the hard part.
People.
Why are people so hard?
I'm sure there's a metaphor in there somewhere,
but today, I am not in the mood for deep thoughts.
Today I'm a downright grouch.

"Is something wrong with your arm?"
Justin asks, swishing his brush around
in a glass of water, then wiping it on a rag.
I let go of my stump, which I have been clenching.
"No. I'm fine," I say.
Justin gives me a look.
Justin and I, during our long stays at the hospital,
we developed a pretty fine-tuned fluff-meter.
Right now I'm feeding Justin fluff, and he knows it.
Justin and I, we prefer the truth.

"My arm is killing me," I admit,
walking in circles and resisting the urge
to kick a paint can clear across the room.
Justin accepts this with quiet empathy.

We both know all too well the agony
of a throbbing stump. I explain to him
about the neuroma, about trying to avoid
surgery by trying natural cures.

"Like what?" he asks. I bite my lip as more spasms
take over. "Heat," I tell him. "Ice. Ultrasound.
Stuff like that."
He leaves the room and returns
with an ice pack and his mother.
She's worried. "Jane? Do you want to lie down?
Do you need me to take you home?"
Now I'm sorry I said anything.
"No, thank you. We want to finish up this part
of the mural today. If I rest a minute,
I should be fine."

She hovers a while, mothering.
Justin fetches us cookies.
When his mom leaves, Justin and I
lean back against his dresser, the plate of cookies
on the floor between us, the ice pack
pressed to my stump. The pain begins to fade.
Justin selects a cookie. He says,
"Maybe you should let the doctor fix your arm.
Even though you're afraid."
I grimace at a fresh stab of pain. "Maybe.

But I'd rather not have an operation, Justin.
I'd rather fix it some other way."
He pats my shoulder. "Okay."
He sounds like he'd like to say more
but is being kind.
"Let's change the subject," I say.
He eats his cookie and thinks. Then he asks,
"Why do you like drawing so much?"

I mull this over. "I'm not sure.
Maybe . . . creating something from nothing?
Learning something new each time I do?
Watching my sketches take on life?
I don't think I could pick one reason.
Everything about drawing is pretty wonderful."

Justin tosses Spot the last of his cookie.
Spot snaps it up and licks the floor intently.
"I've been drawing a lot since our last time together,"
he tells me. I turn to look at him, surprised.
"Yeah? Let me see!"
He pulls a tablet of paper from under his bed.
Soon we are leafing through the pages,
and wonder grows inside of me with each turn.
"Justin, these are great. You are improving with every
drawing! Do you see it?"
He laughs. "Not really. But it's fun.
That vanishing point thing you taught me really helped."

I look them over a bit longer, chuckling to myself.
"Not really?" Isn't that what I said to Mr. Musker,
when he asked if I saw improvement in my own work?
It just goes to show.
We're never as objective as we think we are.
Justin is getting a lot better, and that's all there is to it.
Does that mean that I am, too,
and just don't see it?

"Practice makes perfect," I tell him, closing the pad.
"Keep at it. You're doing *great*."
He grins with pride. "Ready to get back to the mural?"
I stand up and set the ice pack on the dresser. "Yes, I am."
He picks up a brush and I do the same.
Hard or not, the people have to be dealt with
if we want to finish this masterpiece.
And we do.

That's another thing we have in common.
Justin and I, we don't
quit.

Price Tag

"You are *kidding*.
Max *Shannon*?
He's going to be your *tutor*?"
Angie's black-lined eyes are huge.

"I thought he was going to school
in New York or something,"
Trina adds.
"You said you didn't go out there yet,"
Rachel says, confused.
She gives me a quick, searching look.

I dig into my ravioli.
Rachel. Why did I—?
See, this is the problem with lies.
Once you tell a single
crumb of untruth,
you start paying the price.
You have to look people in the eye.
You have to make up *more* lies.
Things unravel.
Quickly.

"I went there after you and I talked,"
I tell her, rearranging my plate.
"I ran into him in the cafeteria."

Rachel accepts this explanation cheerfully.
"Wow. That is so *great,*" she says.
"Jane and Max. Hitting the books!"

Elizabeth makes a loud whistling noise
while Trina says, "Oooooh!"
Angie bats her eyes dramatically,
and Rachel makes a kissy sound.
I glance around at the other tables,
feeling my cheeks burn.
Normally
I would be joking
right along with them.
Today I have zero sense of humor.
In fact, I am dangerously close
to a foul mood.

I'm pretty sure
this is another price
of telling lies.

Skies and Seas

At home
I work on the painting
I plan to enter into the competition.
It's a bright scene:
a sliver of scenery
from Santa Barbara,
painted from memory.

The pier stretches out into the water,
waves roll gently onto the beach,
mountains range across the horizon,
and orange California poppies glitter
from fields far behind rocky outcroppings.
Families play along the pier
and lean over the railings.

It's the most ambitious thing I've ever tried to paint,
and if not for Mr. Musker's help and patience
I would have scrapped it long ago.
Tonight I work on the palm trees,
stubbing layers of light
into the green fronds,
trying to give depth to the shadows beneath.

When I'm done,
I stand back and take stock.
Parts are working; parts are not.

But as I told Justin,
practice makes perfect.

Thankfully,
there's plenty of time
and plenty of paint
to go
before the competition deadline.

He Calls

Max has my phone number.
Mine, riding around on a scrap of paper in his pocket.
He's supposed to call to confirm our first session.
I am wrapping Mabel's front paw in bandages,
practicing my skills on her willing four legs,
when the phone rings.
I bash both shins stumbling into a chair,
and Mabel leaps out of the way,
bandages trailing in a stream.
I snatch up the phone. "Hello?"
"Hi. Jane? This is Max."
"Hello, Max."
"What are you doing?"

Waiting for you to call me.
Even though you probably have a girlfriend.
Even though it's all totally ridiculous.
That's what I'm doing.

"Um, nothing much."

"I was calling about the tutoring.
Did you talk to your mom?"

Goodness, the sound of his voice in my ear
makes me need to sit down. "Yes.
She said it was fine. We're all set."

"Great. Tomorrow still work for you?"
"Okay. I mean, yes. Yes, tomorrow is fine."
"I can come right after swim practice."
"Oh. Okay."
"We have our first meet coming up soon."

Did he pause, just for a moment?
Is there room to jump in, ask him why
he didn't go away to college out east
like I heard he had planned, and if
he is dating anyone? Sarah, perhaps?

"Well . . . see you then," he says.

"Bye, Max."
If there *was* a pause,
if there was a chance to talk,
I blew it.

Next Time

We both hang up,
and after a minute, I catch my breath.
Then I call Rachel.
I relay the conversation for her
word for word.
Rachel sighs. "Jane . . . you should
have asked him about his swim stuff."
I bite my lip. "Oh?"

"*Jane*. Why do you think he even mentioned it?
And saying he has a meet coming up?
He was *hinting*. I bet he wanted you to come to it!"
"You think?"
"*Yes*. Jane. We have *got*
to get you in dating shape.
You are like . . .
way behind on how to talk to boys."

As if I don't know this?
I'm an *idiot* when it comes to boys.
"Rub it in, why don't you," I say.
"I'm a little behind on things, okay?
I was sidelined for a *whole year,*
remember?"
There's a small silence.
"What do you mean?" Rachel asks.

"Did something happen to you last year?"
We both giggle.
It's a joke we use often now,
when the mood needs lightening.

Humor helps. And next time?
Next time I talk to Max,
I won't blow it.
Next time
I'll do better.

Text Messages between Mom and Jane

M: Working late tonight. Will you be okay?

J: Yes.

M: I'll be home around ten. Lock up. OK?

J: Ok. CU later.

M: Love you.

J: Love U, too.

Late Nights

Mom. Working late.
The third time this month.
Not that I'm counting.

This morning,
when she put on her best sweater
and wafted by
in a cloud of perfume,
I knew something was up.

I wonder when I'll meet him.

So What?

So today I took
a little extra time
fixing my hair.

So I straightened up
the living room
before leaving for school.

So I even brushed Mabel
and dusted the furniture.
So what?

It does *not* mean
I did that because Max
is coming here tonight.
It just means —

Well,
you figure it out.

Tuesday at Seven

Rachel calls:
"This is the night, right?"
Angie, too: "Wear your black sweater.
He won't be able to resist!"
Even Trina and Elizabeth send texts:
Call me after Max leaves. Want details. :) — T
Call me later. Tell me everything. — E
Then Mom sends a text:
Working late again tonight.
Sorry for the short notice.
Call if you need me.
See you about 10.

She must have forgotten
Max was coming over tonight
because there's *no way*
she'd leave us alone otherwise.
I don't see any reason to remind her.
Besides, it's kind of nice to have the quiet.
Though that very quiet shatters
to a billion pieces
the moment
the doorbell
rings.

A Lethal Weapon

Shocking. Seeing Max walk around in my home,
leaving a faint trail of chlorine-scented air.
He squats to pet Mabel, who sniffs his shoes.
"What a cute dog," he says. "So fluffy."
She licks him on the nose, and he grins.

Great. My dog has scored a kiss with Max
two seconds after he's walked in.
And what am I doing? Standing around staring,
his coat over my arm.
"You want something to eat or drink?" I ask.
Max stands and shakes his head. "No, thanks."
His tall, broad-shouldered body
seems to deprive the room of oxygen.
"We'll work in here." I lead the way
into the small room off the kitchen.
Max puts his backpack down
and pulls up a chair.
He nods toward the desk by the window.
"Are those your weights?"

I glance over at the pink dumbbells
lying on the desk. "How'd you guess?"
Max says with a smile,
"The pink sort of gave it away.
Though they could have been your mom's.
Or your brother's, for all I know."

We both laugh, and I set books on the table.
"Michael using pink weights. Or pink anything.
That would be the day."
"Hey, I competed in a pink swimsuit once,"
Max says.
I smile. "Seriously?"
He nods. "It was for breast cancer awareness.
The whole team wore pink Speedos."
I busy myself with pencils and paper,
trying to get the image of Max in a Speedo
out of my mind before I start blushing.
Too late. "That's cool."
Max asks, "So — you work out much?"
I take a seat. "I lift weights five times a week.
I'm supposed to keep my muscles strong
in order to compensate for Chuck."
Max squints, confused.
"Chuck? Who's Chuck?"

Oh, for heaven's sake.
That one just slipped out.
"It's what I call my fake arm.
Kind of stupid, huh?"

He laughs again. "You named your arm Chuck?"
"My *fake* arm," I remind him.
"That is fantastic," he says. "I love it."

He puts his elbow on the table
and rests his chin in his hand.
"So, if you're working out five times a week,
I'm guessing you've got some serious strength.
I bet you're like the Hulk or something."

I like the easy way Max talks with me.
He is not timid or nervous
about saying the wrong thing,
about offending or treating me special.
He's just having fun.
"I am so strong, you would not believe it,"
I tell him, somber-faced.
"In fact, my arm has been registered as a lethal weapon
with the state of California."

"Really?" Max takes his chin out of his hand
and puts his palm toward me.
"Let's arm wrestle."

Arm Wrestling

I look at him quickly. *Seriously?*
"Okay, but don't say I didn't warn you."
I grab his hand, and, oh, it's warm,
and something like an electric current
shoots through my entire body.
Sparks ignite
every inch of my being.

"Ready?" Max says. "Go."
I push hard,
and Max pushes back, steadily.
I push harder; Max barely moves.
"Any time now," he says, grinning.
In our efforts, our heads bow,
moving closer together,
closer
and closer.

I jerk my head up. "Spider!"
Max leaps to his feet,
smacks at his shoulder, chest, and arms.
"*Where?* Did I get it? Where?"
He yanks the books up, looking underneath.
He's so funny, all spooked, frantically searching.
I can't help it. I laugh, long and hard.
He narrows his eyes at me.

"Ahhhh . . . the old spider trick."
"I'm sorry," I manage.

"Don't be. All's fair in arm wrestling."
Max opens the science book, becoming studious.
"You do know the penalty for cheating, though."
I shake my head as the giggles die.

"Extra homework."

"I don't even understand the homework I *have*."
Good grief. I'm *whining*.

"That's why I'm here, remember?"
Max takes a pair of glasses out of his shirt pocket
and slides them on,
and though I wouldn't have thought it possible,
he is now more handsome than before.
"By the time the night is over,
you will understand this assignment,
and the extra one I'll give you."
Max turns the page.
"Let's get started," he says.

And so
we do.

Magnetism

"Ferromagnetic substances," I tell him.
"I *beg* you to explain this to me."
"Ah, yes," Max says with a heavy sigh.
"I remember all this. Kind of."
He glances at me sideways.
"I'm kidding." He chuckles.
"Wow. You should have seen your face."
Max cracks his knuckles
and picks up a pen and a pencil.
He holds them so their tips are touching.
"Let's say these two objects
are magnetically attracted to each other,"
he says. "If the pencil is a ferromagnetic substance,
it will remain magnetic even after you take away the pen."

He does so, leaving the thin pencil in midair by itself.
"The pencil does not depend on the pen
to be magnetic." He touches the pencil to my shoulder.
"It could just as easily stick to you.
Or the refrigerator. Or the table. See?"

I nod, slowly understanding.
Max returns the pen to the pencil,
their points touching like a kiss.
"If we apply the pen to the pencil,
we increase the magnetization.
When we increase it

to the highest value it can go
without raising it above the Curie temperature,
it is saturation magnetization.
It is as magnetic as it can get."
He looks at me.
"Understand?"
I nod.
He says, "And the Curie temperature is . . . ?"
That one I remember.
"It depends on the substance."
He beams. "Good. Let's say . . . iron?"
I quickly check my notes.
"770 degrees Celsius."
"Good. Cobalt?"
"1130."
"Good. So . . .
is the Curie point a set number?"
I shake my head. "No?"

"*No* is not a question, Jane.
Confidence. You probably know this
better than you think."
I try again. "*No.*"

"Excellent." Max sits back.
"Now. What's another way of explaining
the Curie temperature?"
I think hard. But I don't know.
Max presses the pencil against my palm.

"Picture that pencil being cooked.
It's getting hotter and hotter and hotter,"
Max adds. He is so close, so near.
Yes, it is getting hotter. Yes, it is.
"The pencil is magnetic," Max says.
"But as it gets hotter, it . . ."
He slowly floats the pen away.

"It loses its magnetism?"
I ask.
He beams. "Bingo!"
I look at the pencil, at the pen,
and it sinks in:
a grain of comprehension.
"So the Curie temperature
is the temperature at which
the substance loses its magnetism?"

"Yes!" Max crows.
"See? You catch on fast.
This is going to be *easy.*"

Easy?
I think about the gigantic textbook
before us.
There is *so much* inside,
and I understand about 2 percent of it.
Easy
is not the word I would choose.

But as I watch Max
patiently leafing through my notes,
hope
is the word
I find.

Silence

As I shower that night,
I think back to our session,
to the final minutes of it,
when his phone lit up,
where it lay on the table by our elbows,
how I glanced at it as it buzzed,
and saw the name
Brittany
in its lighted window.

Max silenced the phone
with a push of a button.
"Sorry, I thought I'd turned that off,"
he'd said, and resumed our lesson,
but not before he'd stared at the phone
for a heartbeat, his brow furrowed.
I could barely concentrate
after that, wondering if Brittany
is Max's girlfriend.

When he left, I watched out the window.
I saw him put his phone to his ear
even before he climbed into his car.
He didn't want to keep Brittany waiting,
I guess. Or perhaps
he was talking to Sarah.
Who knows?

And it's
none of my business.

Slipping into bed,
I hear Mom unlock the front door
and close it again behind her.
She's home from working late.
If that's really where she was.
I don't want to talk to her tonight.
I shut my eyes, pretending to sleep.
My arm begins to ache, and I press it
to stop the throbbing.

A long time later,
Mom tiptoes past the door,
down the hall to her bedroom.

Softly,
she hums.

Glimmer

The next day in science class, Mr. Veckio asks,
"What is the best way to define the Curie point?"

To everyone's surprise,
I raise my hand.
He calls on Matthew instead,
but that's okay. Because I know
that I *know* it.
"Good job," Matthew whispers to me.

Turning in my homework,
with *confidence* for a change,
I find I can't wait for our next session.
Not just because it involves seeing Max again.
But because I like the experience
of understanding.
I like knowing.

As far as
Brittany goes?
I wouldn't mind
knowing
a bit more about that, either.

Perilous

At the clinic,
I lie still while a slim woman
with shiny red hair
applies ultrasound massage
to my residual limb.
The small, buzzing wand
glides across cold, slimy gel
plastered on my stump.
"I like your hair," I tell her.
She beams. "I like yours, too."

At home, I apply heat
in the form of our old heating pad,
which has seen this family
through many backaches,
sprains, and chills.

"Can you feel a difference?"
Dr. Kim asks in a follow-up phone call.
"Not yet," I answer.
I can almost hear him nodding.
"Let's give it more time.
Acupuncture will be our next move
if we don't see improvement."
Oh, boy. *Needles? In my stump?*
The image makes me nauseous.

That night, as usual,
I clean my stump carefully
before going to bed.
Any small wound, even a scrape,
can lead to a major infection, fast.
That's one of the many perils that come
with losing a limb.
The wrenching pain
that catches me off-guard
the next morning?
That's another.

Fumbling for a bag of ice,
I wonder when this process
of "moving on"
will ever end.

Pop Quiz

"Good job, Jane."
Mr. Veckio hands back
the pop quiz.
I stare in disbelief
at the B+
at the top of the paper.

The highest grade
I have ever made
in this class.
Wow.

So it's official.
Tutoring with Max is worth
the torture
I put myself through
every time I think
about

Brittany.

Sand

Today in art, Mr. Musker lets us work on anything we want to.
I begin working on the piece
for the art show. A painting needs texture
to have life. It needs texture
as much it needs depth and light.
Today I need to put grit
into the sand.

However, painting sand
to look like sand instead of liquid mush
is not so easy.
Mr. Musker brings over a scrap of canvas,
wets his own brushes, sits down, and shows me,
step by step, how to "grainify" that beach.
Soon a small cluster of kids gathers around,
watching intently, as he demonstrates.
"I'm going to try that," Nathan says.
"Me, too," says Emily, to everyone's shock.

Dabbing at the painting, I see my careful attempts
to do exactly as Mr. Musker says
result in something the nature of oatmeal.
It's all I can do not to scream.
"Use this for practice," Mr. Musker says,
pushing another scrap of canvas my way.
He pats me on the shoulder as he rises.
"Rome wasn't built in a day."

He moves off to help other students
with their projects. I keep working,
my heart sinking as time runs out
and my painting is *worse* than before.
Thank goodness for the ability
to paint over your mistakes.
And over.
And over.

Rome may not have been built in a day,
but headaches, tension, and short tempers?

They can be built in just forty-seven minutes flat.

Birthday Night

Mom drives Rachel, Elizabeth, and me
to Trina's party, the pink tiered cake
balanced between us in the backseat.
It's pretty much a fabulous work of art,
if I do say so myself . . . all curls and bows
and delicate piping.

At Trina's house,
we deliver the cake to a squealing Trina,
while her mother cries,
"Oh, my goodness. Jane, you are a wonder!
This cake is *gorgeous*."
After thanks and photos, *lots* of photos,
we hurry downstairs to the
cool, brightly lit room in the basement.
We set to work finishing up decorations.
Music is already thumping, filling us with excitement,
and soon the party is officially under way.
Trina is beautiful as always, her hair black and shiny,
her makeup sparkly and bright.
"The red plate is all vegetarian sandwiches,"
Trina tells me. "I wanted you to have
something to choose from."
I give her a hug, seconds before
Kevin scoops her away for a kiss.

Then I spot a group of kids awkwardly
thunking down the stairs, glancing around.
Boys. And Matthew is among them.

Matthew says to me, "Wow, you look nice."
It's sinking in now,
now that I've spent time with Max.
How you should feel
about someone you like.
I have to talk to Matthew
and end whatever it is
we have started up between us.
But not here.
You'd have to be a pig of epic proportions
to break up with someone at a party.
So I say, "Thanks. You do, too."

Matthew motions toward the table.
"Want a soda?"
"Sure." I follow him and notice the way
he looks at Lisa Stine and the way
she looks back at him. *Electric.*
Though she turns away quick,
I am now alive with wonder.
Do they like each other?
Because that would be really great if . . .

Before I can think anymore about that,
Trina and Kevin shout,

"Dance time!" and everyone
crowds onto the floor,
a steaming jumble of elbows and legs
and thumping, bumping music.

I join in,
because it's too late
to get out of the way.

In a Corner

Shadowed pockets make private corners
at the edges of tables laid out with cheese puffs,
sodas, and sandwiches.
Crowds dance, hips swaying,
laughter and shouting drowned out
by the relentless music.
Matthew beckons.
He leads me to one of these dim cocoons.
"Let's take a break," he says loudly.

He pulls me to a lumpy loveseat.
"Having fun?" he says.
He has to speak into my ear
because the music is the level
of crashing mirrors and exploding cars.
"Yes. Are you?" I ask.
He puts his arm along the back of the sofa.
"Jane. We have to talk."
"What about?"
"I think we should stop seeing each other."

I stare. "You do?"
Matthew wipes his palms on his shirt.
"I like you a *lot*. You're really great. But —
I think you're not really into me.
And the thing is, I like someone else, who *is* into me.
And I thought . . . I just thought . . ."

Oh, *thank goodness.*
I rush to speak. "I understand.
It's okay, really."
He waits a second. "Am I wrong?
Do you like me? Because . . ."

"I like you a lot," I tell him.
Even though you are dumping me at a party.
"I think you're a great guy.
But you're right.
I only like you as a friend."
And I know who the "someone else" is,
and her initials are *Lisa Stine.*

It's almost funny how my ego
wants to mess this up for me,
how it wants to be hurt
and rejected and angry.
Almost funny, but not really.
Get a grip, Jane. Good grief.

The booming music stops.
Everyone on the dance floor stumbles to a halt.
"Hang on!" Trina yells. Laughing,
she fumbles with the stereo.
"So you're okay with this?" Matthew asks.
I give him a smile. "Yeah. I am."

He suddenly leans forward
and kisses my cheek.
"See you, Jane."

I watch him walk into the crowd
of people on the floor.
I sigh, get up,
and search for a soda
as the music begins again.

I wonder what Max is doing
right this minute.

8. Go to Prom

Angie applies lipstick at a cracked mirror.
"Too bad Matthew broke up with you.
He was your best shot for prom."
"Angie?" I say. "Sometimes I want to smack you."
Elizabeth calls from the bathroom stall,
"I second that."
Angie drops the lipstick into her bag.
"I'm just saying. Prom is three months away.
You should have a date by now.
You should have a *gown* by now."
"I'm sure you and Scott will have a lovely time,"
I tell her with a serene smile
that I know drives her nuts.

Elizabeth joins us, washes her hands,
primps her hair. "Jim and I
are thinking of getting a limo."
"Oooh, we should go halfsies on that,"
Angie says. "Maybe get Rachel and Tom
in on it, too. And Kevin and Trina."
"That's not *halfsies*," I say, sounding
irritable and left out. "That's fourths."

"Jane, it's *fine* to go to prom alone,"
says Elizabeth. "You should come with us.
I know you don't want to, but . . ."
"Too bad you can't ask Max,"

Angie says. "*That* would be something."
Max is not allowed to come to prom
because he's a college student.
Not that I'd *ever* ask him in a zillion years.
Can you *imagine*?

"Let us know if you change your mind," says Angie.
"And miracles happen — you may still get asked!"
She sounds like we're holding out hope
for a rescue mission on a snowy mountaintop
where I might perish without aid.

"Yeah, maybe," I say, to keep the peace.
And, the reality is, "go to prom"
is on my bucket list for a reason.
It's silly, but . . .
who doesn't want that one magical night,
the beautiful gown,
the delicate flower corsage,
the music, friends, dancing, laughing?
When we leave school,
we'll go on to college, or jobs,
or both. Marriage . . . families . . .
it's all coming. But for now?
For now there's prom.
Is it so wrong
to want that?

Letter from Lucy
San Diego, California

Dear Jane,

I am doing a report for school about challenges and handicapped people. I can't imagine how awful it must have been to have been attacked by a shark! I am glad you are okay now, though. Would you answer some questions for me for my report?

Also, I just read about a man who is a quadruple amputee, and he swam the English Channel. He says that if you put your mind to it, you can accomplish anything. Do you agree? Have you accomplished the things you want to?

Best wishes,

Lucy

Without a Map

In science class, I am once again lost.

"Jane? Do you want to answer that one?"
Mr. Veckio asks.

Yes I do, Mr. Veckio.
But I have no clue.

"Um . . . particles of light?"

Mr. Veckio shakes his head.
"No. Anyone else?"

I take notes. I highlight things
in the textbook.
I effortlessly visualize a big fat F
hovering over my report card.
And I count the hours
until Tuesday.

Strange Boy

"Hey, wait a minute.
Weren't you supposed
to have your first tutoring session
last week?"

I glance up from my desk,
where I'm shading the shadows
under Max's jawline in a charcoal sketch.
Mom stands in the doorway
in her nightgown, a magazine in one hand.
"Um . . . yes." I casually hide the drawing
under a blank piece of paper.

She thinks a minute.
"One of the nights I worked late.
Was that the day?"
"Yes."

Mom sighs. "If I ever forget again,
remind me. Understand?
I don't want you here alone
with some strange boy."

"He's not strange."
I say it without thinking,
and by the expression on her face,
I see that's the wrong thing.

"Okay, I will. Things went fine, Mom.
It's going to be a real help."

She hesitates, then smiles.
"I'm glad, sweetie.
I know this means a lot to you,
and you have your mind set on a good grade
in that class. If anyone can do it, you can."

"Thanks, Mom."

She slips off down the hallway.
I hear the creak of her bed
as she settles in.

She hasn't worked late in a few days.
I don't know if this means anything
regarding her dating life
or not.

What I *do* know?

Tuesday is fast approaching,
and with it another evening with Max.
I can hardly wait.

Rewind

The ultrasound lady
now has purple hair.
"I like your hair," I tell her. Again.
"Thanks. I like yours, too," she says.
Again.
She seems to not remember
we had this same exact conversation
last time.

And we've had this exact same
session. The slimy gel,
the wand rolling all over my stump,
the hot compresses at home,
and the total
lack of results.

I roll my stump in a bowl of rough, dried beans
to desensitize it, take two aspirin,
and go to bed,
my flesh and bones
crackling
with invisible
flames.

Studies with Max

"No tricks tonight," Max says.
Thumb up, he holds out a fist.
"Just good old-fashioned thumb wrestling."
I laugh, then check. He's serious. "Oh."
He wiggles his thumb. "Come on. I need closure."

My thumb is ridiculously small
next to his. Giggles threaten to bubble up.
I try to bite them down, but Max hears them.
"This is critical," he says.
"One, two, ready, go!"
His thumb catches mine and pins it to his fist.
He throws his hands over his head.
"Yes! The winner!"

I shake out my thumb, laughing.
"You take *pride* in that? It's hardly equal."
He drops his arms. "You do have a pretty small thumb."
"Genetics. What can I say?"
"Ah, back to science," Max says, pulling a pen
from his shirt pocket. "Tonight
we review the periodic table. Right?"
I swallow. "Right."
And we do. We study.
And in the process of studying science,
I also study Max.

I learn he has long dark lashes,
extremely neat handwriting,
a fondness for fruit gum,
and (because I dropped a pencil and had to get it)
shoelaces that had been broken and knotted
into submission, over and over, in a big
snarly mess.

"Should I get us a snack?" I ask when we finish.
Good grief. I sound like someone's mother.
But Max is agreeable. "Sure."

He marvels over the oatmeal cookies I've made.
"Wow. You are an excellent baker," he says.
"My mom used to make these from scratch.
I really miss them. And believe me,
when I try to re-create them,
it's a disaster of epic proportions."

"I'm glad you like them."
It takes considerable restraint
not to offer to make him cookies
every day for the rest of his life.

Max balances a pencil on the end of his finger.
"Bet you can't do this."

"Sure I can," I tell him, straight-faced.
"I do it all the time."

Soon we are having a battle of pencil balancing,
and I'm laughing harder than I have
in ages. When the hall clock chimes nine, we stop.
"Guess I better get going," Max says.
"Good luck on your quiz. Go over our notes
a few more times. Okay?"
"Okay." I watch him pack up. "Thanks, Max."
He pauses at the door, his backpack over his shoulder.
His grin is dazzling. "See you soon."

I close the door, still warm from laughing.
I push the hair off my face. Study? Yes.
Bake cookies for our next session?

You bet.

Up and Down

"Happy birthday!" my friends cry,
surrounding the pizza, which has
seventeen candles stuck in the cheese.
I blow them out, and laugh when they applaud.
"Dig in," I tell them, and we grab slices.

Spring is upon us. March has come in like a lamb,
all warm weather and sunny skies.
And now here I am, another year older.
My friends pile presents at me.
I am so lucky to have them in my life.

But the next day
a black mood follows me around for hours.
I soak in the tub, read a new book,
bury myself in homework and science notes.
Nothing chases it away.

Three weeks pass.
Tutoring is fantastic. Max
makes everything understandable.
"You're smart," he tells me.
"So *determined*." He grins at my eye roll.
"When you don't understand something,
it makes you mad. You work hard to get it.
I like that."

The room shines like a million-watt light
with those words. The rest of the week,
I practically dance on air. Michael,
home for a visit, notices.
"Uh-oh," he says. "It's a guy, isn't it?"
I throw a pillow at him.
"Just make sure he's not an *ax murderer,*"
Michael quips before ducking into his room.

Three weeks pass, and my paintings
get tighter, crisper. With Mr. Musker's guidance,
all of my work steadily climbs
the rungs of my expectations.
The exultation is like a drug;
I want more and more and more.
I work into the early hours of the mornings,
sketch pads piling up on the floor.

Three weeks pass, and
the flare-ups
of excruciating arm-twisting pain
go on and on and on.
"They're coming more frequently,"
Mom says one night
as I clutch my arm in agony.
Thanks for pointing that out, Mom.
Really helpful.
"Honey, maybe we should
consider that surgery," she says.

"We?" I sound harsh,
but I don't care.
Pain makes you do harsh things;
it makes you mean.
"There is no *we* in surgery.
Just me. Under the knife.
I'm not doing it.
I don't want any more of that stuff.
Ever."

Mom presses her lips in that thin line
she's been wearing lately.
I don't care.
And the next night,
when she has to work late
again, I almost blurt out,
"So what's his name, Mom?
Why on earth don't you just come clean?
Are you ashamed of me?
Is that why you haven't brought him over?"

Naturally, I don't.
I don't want to open any
cans of worms right now.

But it's funny
how I can feel so good
one minute and so bad
the next. And how I can't

reason, control, or talk myself
out of my feelings. *Any* of them,
even the irrational ones.

Is this all part of growing up?
Because if it is,
I can't wait
to get it over with.

In-Box

March is nearly over.
I've spent every day of it
checking my in-box a million times a day.
Nothing.
But today, suddenly,
there they are,
responses from all four of the schools I applied to.
I click on one, two, three, and,
with growing amazement, four.

Michael, reading over my shoulder, whoops.
"You made it!" He snatches me up in a hug and spins
me around the room. "Congratulations!"
"What school?" Mom asks, trotting into the room.
"Which one?"
I feel my eyes wet with tears of excitement,
of relief. *"All of them."*

"All four?" Mom shrieks. She punches her fists
into the air. *"Yes!"* She piles into us,
and we clench in a group hug.

First things first, I remember telling Justin,
back when we began that mural.
I chose my schools. I applied to them.
I made it in. To *all* of them.

The next step? Choosing the one I want to commit to.
The thought of making that decision
nips at this happy feeling.
But then the elation returns,
and I nod *yes* to Mom's offer
of a celebratory dinner out.
This could have turned out differently.
I could be feeling limited in my choices right now.
Let's face it. Given what happened to me
I could be *dead* right now.
Instead, at the moment, it feels like
the sky is my limit.

Decisions are hard, yes.
But oh, how grateful I am
to have decisions
to make.

Two Kids

The slight lift of a girl's hair, indicating a breeze.
The captivating pattern on a butterfly's back.
Two dogs (that both look like Spot) frolicking over a hill.
A miniature world of ladybugs,
inchworms, a friendly garter snake,
and a turtle, hidden among leafy clover
along the edge of the river.
Today, finally, after many hours and many breaks,
our mural, in all its sunshiny
glory, is done.

Justin and I stand before it,
the April air light through the window,
and contemplate our work.
"What do you think?" I ask him.
"Did it come out just like the sketch?
The way we imagined it would?"
His eyes shine. He shakes his head.
"No. It came out *better.*"

We fist-bump. Then we begin
putting lids on the paint. After
everything dries, Justin's parents
can finally move all this out of here—
the drop cloths, the ladder, the supplies.
In time, the room will stop smelling like paint.
And for as long as he lives here,

Justin will have a park at his side,
a park that is always sunny and inviting,
his own private place to slip away to
while he lies in bed.
"I'm a little jealous," I tell Justin as we clean up.

"Maybe you should paint one on *your* wall,"
he says. "I'd help you."
I laugh. "That's an idea. Maybe.
If I end up staying close to home for college,
maybe I will."

He grows quiet at the mention, and
I'm sorry I brought it up. We spend a minute
placing paint cans in a box. After we finish our work,
I look at him. "I put something special in the mural.
Something small that I didn't tell you about.
I did it while you were on the phone with your grandma.
I bet you can't find it."

Justin's smile is big enough to light the room.
He hurries to the wall and stands close.
"What is it? Is it another Spot? Another soccer ball?
An extra butterfly?" He stretches his neck to look high.
"That orange bird? No, wait. We already had that bird.
Is it . . . ? Um, is it — ?" he breaks off, silently looking.
Finally he huffs and turns to me. "I don't see it."
I grin at him. "I know. But you will."
His eyes grow wide as I pick up my jacket and purse.

"Aren't you going to tell me what it is?"
I slip on the jacket. "No."
"But I want to know!"
"Then you better look. Believe me, Justin.
You'll see it. Nothing gets by you."
He zeroes in on the clumps of tiny people
we have painted, walking a path far at the edge of the park.
"Is it someone in here? Give me a hint."
I waggle my five fingers at him. "Bye!"
He runs over. "Bye."
Then he gives me a tight hug.
I lean my chin against the top of his head,
touched and honored.
Justin is getting older now,
and he normally squirms away from hugs.

"Thank you," he says into my shoulder.
"You're welcome, Justin. I'm glad you like it."
He pulls away, still grinning. "I *love* it."
I survey the mural once more,
with fresh eyes this time.
Wow. You know what?
It really *did* come out nice.
Very nice.
Not bad for two kids
who never painted something so huge before.

Not bad at all.

PROM NIGHT!

Saturday, May 10
7 pm–midnight
SENIORS: Tickets go on sale APRIL 11!
Available at the front office.

FOOD! MUSIC! LIVE BAND! DANCING!

ROCK YOUR SENIOR PROM!

Hold the Phone

Mom calls to me from downstairs.
"Phone call for you."
I hurry from my room. *Is it Max?*
Is he cancelling our next session?
"Hello?"
"Hi, Jane? This is Josh."
A moment of silence follows as I churn
the contents of my brain, trying to locate Josh.

"From your triage class."
"Oh!"
Laughing Boy.
What is he doing calling me?
How did he even get my number?
"I got your number from my aunt.
Lindsey? From the hospital?"
I sit down. "Lindsey is your *aunt?*"
"Yeah. She asked me about the class,
and I mentioned you, and she knew who you were.
I guess you volunteer at the hospital."
"Yes . . . she's great. I had no idea you were related."
"I just moved here a few months ago.
I go to the same school as you."
"Oh. How do you like it?"

"I like it. I really like Mr. Musker.
He's my favorite teacher."

"Mine, too."
"Hey. Would you like to go to prom with me?"

"Prom?" I repeat it as though the word were unclear.
But I heard him. *Prom.*
Prom — which is rapidly approaching.
"I should clear one thing up," Josh says quickly.
"I already have a girlfriend.
She lives back in Modesto, where I just moved from.
She can't come out for the prom. So . . . I'm asking you.
But I'm only asking as a friend. You know what I mean?"
Do I ever.
"And your girlfriend is okay with that?" I ask.
Josh laughs. "Yeah. She told me it was fine,
as long as we don't do any slow dances together."

I inhale deep, my mind whirling.
"I would love to go to prom with you, Josh."
I can hear him exhale. "Good. Wow. I'm so glad.
We'll have a blast."
"I'll introduce you to my friends," I say.
He sounds like he's smiling. "Great. I'd like that."

I get his phone number, tucking the phone under my ear
and writing it down. I make a promise to look for him
at school. We agree to split the cost of the tickets.
"And my friends are going in a limo," I tell him.
"Want me to check and see if we can join them?"
"Sure," he says. "That would be great."

We chat a minute more, with Josh laughing
freely and easily like he did back in triage class.
I like his sense of humor.
"If you get a head injury while we're there,"
he says, "I'll know just what to do." He pauses.
"I'll ask you who's the president."

We laugh about that one.
When I hang up, I stand there,
mixed emotions swirling
in my chest. I'm going to prom.
With a nice guy. Who just wants to be friends.

Nothing wrong with that.

Is there?

Inferno

Drying off from the shower,
oh—
a swarm of invisible bees
buries into the end of my stump
all at once.

I have to sink to the floor
to catch my breath
and wait
for a wave of nausea
to pass.

It does, quickly,
but the trail of fire
left behind
across my skin,
inside my bones,
and threaded through tissue
will not be put out

no matter what
I try.

Shopping

One thing about Angie. She doesn't mess around.
When it comes to a fashion emergency?
You want her in your court.
"This afternoon," she says.
"We'll go to the same place I got my dress."
"I don't have a ton of money," I warn her.
Angie is already waving me off.
"They have dresses in all price ranges,"
she says, sounding like a catalog. "And shoes.
We have to find shoes. And makeup. Tell you what.
Come to my house on prom night. *I'll* do your makeup."

"Okay." I put down my peanut butter sandwich.
I'm already in over my head.
And I can't help but worry.
Will I look silly in a gown? With half an arm?

That afternoon we stuff ourselves into a fitting room —
me, Rachel, Angie, Trina, and Elizabeth.
Everyone pushes gowns at me.
"Jane, you have to try this one."
"Come on, Jane,
this one matches your eyes."
"Oh, my gosh. You would *love* this one."

Gown after gown goes on, then *off,*

my hair becomes a ratted, tangled mess,
and soon I am sick of seeing myself in my underwear
in the full-length mirror between glittery dresses.
Every gown is wrong, and hope fades.

Then I grab the last dress slung over the chair.
It's one dress that *I* picked out, a pale blue sleeveless
number, with tiny, sparkling beads
shimmering across the top and scattered along the hem.
I stroke the silky soft bodice.
"Let me try this one."

It settles over my hips like a glove.
One look in the mirror, and I know.
"Oh, wow," Elizabeth says.
"That is *gorgeous.*"
"Jane, you're so beautiful," Rachel whispers.
Angie cocks her head,
studies me up and down, then nods
her approval. "Bingo."

I smile into the mirror.
I don't see a girl with half an arm.
I see a *girl.*
She needs a hairbrush,
but overall?
She's not so bad-looking.
She's flushed and smiling.

And she's in a beautiful,
shimmery dress.
That's all. A girl.
In a dress.

For once, I agree with Angie.

Bingo.

Text Messages between Michael and Jane

M: Hey, Li'l Sis. Mom says you're going to the prom.

J: Yep.

M: She says you look "so grown-up" in your gown.

J: Ugh. You know how Mom is.

M: I just wanted to warn you. Mom cried when I got ready to go to prom. She took a million pictures of me in my tux, then she cried all over the place. I almost didn't want to go anymore.

J: Great. Something to look forward to. That may not happen. Mom is all into her mystery boyfriend she thinks she's hiding from me.

M: Oh, yeah. Any word on that?

J: Not much.

M: She probably wants to see if it's going anywhere before bringing it up. Why have a big talk about a boyfriend if she just ends up breaking up with him, right?

J: Hmm. You sound like you have experience in that department. So who are you dating?

M: Don't go there. Besides, you want to tell me about this prom date? Hmm?

J: He's just a friend. We barely know each other.

M: Nice. The stuff dreams are made of. Well . . . enjoy your prom. I'm sure Mom will e-mail me a picture or two.

J: Thanks so much for the chat. It's been ever so helpful.

M: Bye-bye now.

J: Bye.

Letter from Ryan
Hollywood, California

Dear Jane,

I am writing to ask if you would be willing to send me an autograph. My mom has followed your story since it happened, and she just read an update about you in a magazine. She talks about you sometimes, and how inspiring you are. She says you are going to go into nursing. She says it's one of the most noble things she ever heard.

Her birthday is next week, and I know she'd love an autograph. So would you please send me one? For her?

Thank you!

Ryan

Nobility

Mr. Musker helps me figure out
how to place shadows on the sand
and how to give dimension to the mountains
in the background of my painting.
"Jane, this is outstanding,"
he tells me, polishing his glasses.
"You really have done something here."
I wipe the brushes on cloth
and begin putting the paint away.
"Thanks. I couldn't have done it without you."

Our after-school sessions have really paid off.
The piece will be ready in time for the competition.
And not just ready, but *done*.
When I look it over,
I don't wish I'd done anything different.
It's exactly how I pictured it in my head —
the water glinting with sunlight,
the clouds, heavy and white,
the people,
both harshly lit and heavily shaded
in the bright sunshine.

"Have you thought any more about art school?"
Mr. Musker asks.

Only every day.
"Yes. I have. I can't decide yet.
Nursing school is very tempting, too."
Mr. Musker shakes his head.
"I shouldn't try to influence you.
But you know
which one I hope you pick, right?"
"Yes."

Silence falls as we put away
crusted tubes of paint,
throw out crinkled wads of paper towels,
and empty glasses of black paint water.
"Let's just say you pursue art training," Mr. Musker
continues, setting the glasses into the classroom sink.
"What do you see yourself doing with an art degree?
Landscapes? Gallery work?"
"I'm not sure," I tell him. "I've thought about
a lot of stuff. Illustration? Portraiture?"
I frown. "It all sounds good . . . but at the same time,
nothing sounds quite right.
I guess I need to give it more thought."
"And time," he says cheerfully.
"You'll have that, in art school . . .
plenty of time to find what you are drawn to most."
We grin at the pun, but I let his words
comfort me. Time. It's a reassuring idea.

Mr. Musker laughs and helps me hitch the bag
onto my shoulder. "I'll stop pushing now.
Nursing is a fine and noble choice as well."

I tell him good-bye, and I head outside,
dialing Mom to tell her I'm ready to be picked up.
Noble?
So true. Doctors, nurses . . . they *are* noble.
Such a shame that someone who makes art
does not usually qualify
for such a distinction.
I wouldn't hesitate to call Picasso,
Rembrandt, and Vermeer
noble.
Would the rest of the world?
Would all those people who write to me,
who sing my praises for
becoming a nurse?

I'm not so sure.

Studying

After dinner
Mom and I clean up the kitchen.
"That painting is gorgeous,"
Mom says for the third time.
We both stare at it,
where it rests on the side table,
propped against the wall.
"Thanks," I tell her.
"I have to enter it into the competition this week.
I can't believe I finished early."

I glance at the clock. Seven p.m.
The doorbell rings, right on cue.
Mom says, "I'll get it,"
and I let her, hanging back for a second
to put away the last of the silverware.
I listen to them talk to each other,
my pulse picking up speed
at the sound of Max's voice.

They exchange small talk
as they walk into the kitchen.
"I hope you two have a good session,
Mom says. "I'll be in the living room
if you need me."
She gives me a look I can't quite read.

Then she takes the newspaper
and is gone.

I fix my eyes on Max,
his sweatshirt hugging
his big shoulders,
his hair curling at his neck.
Max doesn't move.
He stares at the painting,
his eyes wide.

Remind Me of Something

"Wow." His voice is quiet.
"Did someone in your family make that?"
I come closer. "Yeah. I did."
He stares at me. "No way."
He drags his eyes back to the painting.
"I knew you liked art—I remember
you mentioning it last year.
But I had no idea . . ."
He shakes his head.
"Wow."

"We'll work in here tonight,"
I tell Max as I pull the place mats from the table.
He helps me, carefully moving
the salt and pepper shakers.
"How'd you do on the quiz?"

"Great," I tell him. "But since then . . ."
"Back on a different planet?" Max asks.
"Where they speak a different language
and you have no clue what they're talking about?"
"That's it! How did you know?"
"That's how I am with social studies," Max says.
"I never could get it right."
I realize I have no idea what Max is studying at school.
"Psychology," he says
when I ask.

That is exactly not what I expected. "Why?"
Max pulls a chair up to the table.
"Oh, lots of reasons. It's fascinating.
And it's a great way to help people with their lives.
People who really need it. You know?
Adults. Kids. Families."
Suddenly he says,
"Hey, remind me of something."
I look up, and his long-lashed eyes are so close,
his gaze so intense.
"Why do you want to be a nurse
instead of an artist?"
He points to the painting.
"I mean, being a nurse is fantastic.
But if I could paint like that,
I'd . . . I think I'd have to do *that*."

"Oh, well, that's nice of you to say, but . . ."
"I'm not trying to be nice,"
Max says earnestly. "That is *really good*.
You're not someone who just likes to draw.
You're very talented.
I'm surprised you're even *considering*
not going to art school."

"Me, too,"
I hear myself say.

In the gap of air
and time
and space
that follows,
I am silent
with surprise.

Max just nods, as though what I said
makes any sense at all,
when here we are working hard
so I can pass science
and maybe go to nursing school.

He looks at me and says,
"I understand."

Well.
That makes
one of us.

Muddy Waters

"I don't mean to pry, I'm just wondering,"
Max continues. "You seem to love art,
and you're obviously really good at it.
So why . . . ?"

"Nursing matters," I hear myself say.
What is this?
I'm removed from my own vocal cords?
I clear my throat, clear my head.
"It's a chance to do so much *good,*
you know? Besides, I doubt I . . ."

I stop myself in time.
Good grief. I almost said it out loud.
I almost said:
I doubt I was spared from death
just so I could go back to painting,
as though nothing happened.

And thinking about this,
the voice goes on, in my head,
a string unraveling:
I doubt I was put through this ordeal
so I could hide behind a canvas
instead of helping others get through their own ordeals.

I doubt I lived
so I could work in a lonely sunny studio
surrounded by paints and pastels,
rather than on the front line
with trauma, heartbeats, and need.

I doubt I could call the decision
to be an artist
unselfish.
Not now,
not after all that's happened.
Think of the letters, after all.
Think of the people.
Think of what they say.
What would they say if I changed paths?

I snap out of it. I regard Max.
"You know what? I think I'll get us
some drinks."
Max nods.
I wonder if his studies in psychology
give him magical powers,
an insight into what I'm really saying
or not saying.
I wonder if he thinks I'm insane.
Stop that, Jane, I think
as I pour iced tea into glasses.
Stop being so weird.

I take a deep breath.
I decide we're starting this evening over.
Free of discomfort
and awkward questions
and bumbling non-answers.

I put the glasses on a tray,
pick it up with my left hand,
and leave the kitchen.

I leave the lingering questions
behind.

Swim Meet

We've finished our studying;
now we're lingering, sharing stories and jokes.
"I don't think I've ever met a girl
who likes the Three Stooges,"
Max says. "Fascinating."
"I love the one with the haunted house,"
I tell him, "don't you?"
"It's a classic!" Max stretches.
"Well, I have to get going.
I have to swim early in the morning."

He begins gathering his things.
Rachel's words leap to mind.
Next time.
Show an interest.
"Are you practicing with the team tomorrow?"

"No, I'm just getting my laps in
before classes."
"Sounds fun."
"Yeah. I have to get there at six a.m.
to get my workout in before class."

"Wow, six o'clock in the morning. That's early."
"*Too* early?" he asks. "Because I was wondering
if you wanted to come out, swim with me.

We could get something to eat in the cafeteria after,
and I could run you to school.
I'll have you there before the first bell, I promise."

My lips turn dry. *Don't lick them, Jane.*
You'll look like a salivating wolf.
"That would be fun," I tell him.
"But I'm not much of a swimmer."

Truth is I was a *great* swimmer.
But I haven't swum since that gruesome day,
the day I met the shark.
I'm not much in a hurry to get back into the water.
In fact, I haven't even set a toe in a pool
since the attack. So who knows?
Maybe I've forgotten how to swim.
And do I really want to find out what it's like
to swim with half an arm?
Do I want to make that discovery in front of Max?
No.

Max seems disappointed.
"Oh. Well, that's okay."
"I could come watch," I tell him.
I could watch all day.
He looks surprised.

"Really? You'd want to do that?
I mean, it's early. It's just swimming."

And it's you, I think.
"Swimming and *breakfast,* remember?"
He laughs.
"I forgot. Yeah, breakfast.
No sausage or bacon, right?
We'll find you some nice eggs
and lettuce leaves or something."

We hold each other's gaze for a moment.
His eyes are so *bright.*
"All right, then. See you at the pool at six a.m."
"I'll ride my bike over."
"Great. I can throw it in the car
and take you to school."
And just like that, the plans are made.
A sort-of date.
A sort-of swimming date.
Even though I don't plan to swim.

Six a.m. has never sounded better.

A College Boy

I ask Mom about tomorrow.
My fingers are mentally crossed.
If she says no, then I have to call Max and back out.
"I'm not sure about this,"
Mom says reluctantly.
"He's a college boy, Jane."

"I know."
"He seems like a nice kid," Mom says,
as though confessing.
Something about her expression
makes me ask, "Have you met him before?"

She folds up the newspaper
and begins tidying the living room.
"It took me a while to place him.
Tonight I realized that I've seen him
several times in the past at the drugstore.
With his dad."
She pauses.
"Has he mentioned his dad?"

I shake my head.
Mom sighs. "His dad is —
well, I guess he's got Alzheimer's or is mentally ill.
He's not altogether *there,*
and he's not a nice man.

The few times I've run into them,
Max has been picking up prescriptions
for his dad, and the dad is just—
well, *awful* to him. And everyone else.
And Max is so *patient*. And kind.
That's why I recognized him.
He really stayed in my mind.
I don't know a thing about them,
but it seems like the father
should be in a home by now.
A few years ago, I saw him with his wife.
He treated her the same way.
I wonder what she thinks of all this."

I sit down. A mental image of
Max's home life is coming to mind.
"His mom is dead," I say.
"She died of cancer a couple of years ago."
"Oh." Mom sits down, too,
her brow knitted in concern.
"Does he have any brothers or sisters?"
"No."
Mom sighs again. "Poor kid.
I bet he's all alone with that man,
trying to take care of him."

I think back
to the vague murmurs at school
last year, of Max winning a swim scholarship

to a college back east. I think about the day
we met at the cafeteria, when I asked him,
"Do you go to school here?"
And the expression on his face
when he answered,
"Yeah. I go here."

Regret? Resentment?
Did he give up his scholarship
to a better school to stay with his dad?
I don't know.
That's not something
you just ask somebody —
details about their senile father
and whether or not they live at home
because they need to,
not because they want to.

"Tell you what," Mom says abruptly.
"I'll drive you to swimming tomorrow.
I'll have breakfast in the cafeteria
while you're doing that.
When you're done, I'll take you to school
and go on to work. I don't have to be there
until ten anyway."

Oh! She said yes,
and I am *so happy*
that I don't dare to negotiate.

I just say, "Thanks, Mom,"
and leave quickly, before she changes her mind.

Back in my room,
as I change for bed,
I think about Max,
cheerful, positive,
humorous Max,
and his ailing father
who is not nice to him.

I wish I could help.

Not Tonight

Later that night,
Mom pauses by my bedroom door.
"Jane, there's something
I've been wanting to talk to you about."
I put down my colored pencil,
alarmed. That tone of voice.
Oh, dear. This is it.
This is where she tells me
she has found someone
and that he's coming over for dinner
and they're getting married
and everything is going to change.
Right?

"I . . ." Mom begins,
and then
mercifully,
wonderfully,
her phone rings.

She pulls it from her pocket,
frowns, and says,
"Have to answer this, honey. It's work."

She leaves, and
like a coward,
I put on my pajamas

and dive under the covers.
When she returns
several minutes later,
I am a lump in the dark,
pretending to sleep.

Soon
her footsteps fade away.

Late-Night Texts between Jane and Rachel

J: Am going to meet Max tomorrow for his morning swim at the college! :)

R: OMG. You took my advice, right? You picked up on a hint?

J: Yes. I did better this time.

R: Great! Will you swim too? Wear your blue suit.

J: No swim. Don't want wet hair before school. We are meeting at 6 a.m.

R: Wow. That's early! Can't wait for details. Have fun!

J: I will!

Cage

I thread my way past people leaving the building.
I can hardly wait to see Max.
And, yes, it has crossed my mind that I will be seeing him
in a Speedo.
Hurrying along, my flip-flops flapping,
I breeze up to the heavy doors
of the pool house.
Stepping through the doorway,

I enter another world.
Everything
is so . . . large.

The curved ceiling is so high, so far out of reach;
blinding white lights dangle like diamonds from dark
metal beams.
Air is the biggest thing in this room,
heavy, damp air that
hangs over rows of bleachers
and rolls across the pool itself.

In marked-off lanes,
people swim laps,
their bodies churning up wakes of white foam.
The sound of splashing
engulfs me.
As I watch, two sleek-bodied swimmers

dive from blocks into the water
and disappear into it
as though swallowed.

So much water.
It stretches out
like a vast desert,
a desert with a wet and rippling
surface.
The sight of it is like a smack in the face;
I have not stood this *close* to so much water
since that day
nearly two years ago,
when I walked into the ocean a normal girl
and came out forever changed.

Icy terror washes over my insides,
and my heart begins to thud.
Sweat breaks out along the small of my back.
I stare at the bobbing heads,
thrashing bodies,
and I see
fins—
fins, everywhere.
I see people drowning.
I see myself
drowning

and clawing
and spouting blood
into the red water.

I see myself dying.

Run.

I have to get out of here.
I have to see sunlight
and dirt and pavement
and nothing wet,
nothing at all.

"Jane?"
Dimly I am aware I have just run past Max,
who I think is holding a towel or something.

"I have to go!"
I call it over my shoulder
because I can't look back.
I don't stop
until I am outside
in the blinding California sunshine.
Only then,
leaning over from a wave of dizziness,
do I catch my breath.

"Hey, Jane? Are you all right?"
I swivel my head and peer up at Max.
He is sideways and definitely holding a towel.
I straighten, slowly,
and, slowly, the world stops spinning.
"I'm sorry," I croak.

All I can think of is it's so early.
It's so damn *early,* and I told Max
that I would meet him here,
that I would put my feet in the water
and time his laps.
Imagine what he's thinking right now?
"Max, this is the first time I've set foot
near water
since . . ."

His face slips from confused
to shocked.
He reaches for my arm,
the arm that would be closest to him,
if it were still attached to my body.
He puts his hand on my back instead.
"Jane, I had no idea.
I never even thought . . ."
He rubs his other hand over his eyes.
"How could I have not even thought . . . ?"

I don't need Max
blaming himself
for my hang-ups. "It's okay.
I didn't know that I'd — I'm sorry.
I have to go."
I put my head down and start walking.
Good, Jane. Walk away from the amazing guy
you had a date with this morning.
Because sitting next to a pool is too big a price to pay
for time with Max.

"Wait. I'll get my car," Max calls.
I shake my head.
"It's okay. My mom is here."
I am cold all over,
and hot at the same time,
and I think I may never get over
embarrassing myself this way.
I am the stupidest person
ever.

I thought I had moved on.
Turns out I haven't.

Lied

Mom doesn't say anything
about my aborted swim date this morning.
You know why?
Because halfway to the cafeteria,
I took a detour.
I went and sat in our car
for an hour, grateful that it was unlocked.
Then, at seven, I went and got Mom.
And, yes, I acted like
I did meet Max and that all went fine,
and that I did not
freak out
and nearly climb the walls.
In other words,
I lied.

I didn't want Mom to worry.
I didn't want her thinking
that it was time for me
to go back to therapy or something.
I don't want her to think
she has to keep on fixing me.
Forever.
You know what I mean?

Well. Okay.
The truth is . . .

I really, *really*
didn't want to talk about it.
So . . . honestly?
I lied for my own benefit.

And when I got to school,
and my friends were giggling
and asking for details?
I lied to them, too.
I told them my morning with Max was fine,
it was fun, and it was no big deal.

Yep.
Guess lying is one thing
that is getting
easier
and easier.

Letter from Ashton
Canyon Country, California

Dear Jane,

    My name is Ashton. I am forty years old. I was born without one of my hands. I don't remember ever having two hands, of course, so I don't know what it's like to actually lose one. I do remember going through a period when I was young where I felt left out and wondered why I had to be different from everyone else.

    I know I'm not supposed to say that; mostly when you hear about people like me you hear about how they never pity themselves, and they never have any regrets, and they never have any troubles. Well, sorry to say it, but back then, there were times I did feel sorry for myself. I love basketball, and the reality is, I never could play as well as my friends, though I was extremely good. At times I felt self-conscious around girls because of my arm. To say I never wished I'd just been born with two hands like everyone else would be stretching it. My point is, the article made it sound like you were doing fine, but I wanted to write and say, if you ever have a day where you are angry or unhappy with the way things are, that's okay. It's understandable. Not everyone has to be sunshine all the time.

    Having said that, I do hope that the rest of the article is true, and that you are moving on with your life and finding ways to do all the things you want to do. Anyway, just wanted to write and say, from one lefty to another, best of luck. And I hope you have a long, happy life.

    Ashton

Entering

Life goes on, and deadlines arrive,
even when it seems the world should stop
out of respect for a shattered self-esteem.
Last night I did not sleep.
I pictured Max's confused face,
growing smaller as I ran from him.
When I got up in the morning, the first thing I saw,
in my mind's eye, was all that water at the pool.
But it's Thursday. And it's time to turn in
my painting for the art competition.

"Jane! I'm so glad to see you,"
Mrs. Foxe, the assistant principal, says.
She handles the art show every year;
a panel of five teachers are the judges.
Mr. Musker is not one of them.
He says he can't be impartial.

"I'm glad to see you, too,"
I say to Mrs. Foxe, holding up my painting.
"I'm entering this in the show."
She claps her hands like a child.
"Wonderful! I am so glad to see you
back at it. And oh, my goodness,
isn't that *lovely*!" She sighs.
"I am so glad *I'm* not a judge this year.
I have seen a lot of fantastic pieces this morning!"

Behind me, two girls crowd close,
each carrying her own work of art.
"Wow," says one girl. "That is so good."
"Thanks." I admire her watercolor,
and her friend's mosaic. "Those are really nice."

"Thank you," they say,
and I make room for them,
leaving my painting in the care of Mrs. Foxe,
leaving the room filled with the familiar mix
of hope, anticipation, and nerves.
They say competition is not always healthy,
but I like it. Thinking of Mr. Musker
and the help he gave me,
the encouragement,
the support — it's *right*
to be here, and to be hopeful.
Hopeful — in spite of yesterday's disaster.

"See you at the show next week!"
Mrs. Foxe calls after me.

I turn back and wave.
"I'll be there."

Phone Call from Justin to Jane

Justin: Hi.

Jane: Hi, Justin. What's up?

Justin: I think I found the thing you hid in the painting.

Jane: Oh, yeah? What is it?

Justin: A chipmunk.

Jane: A chipmunk?

Justin: Yeah. By the turtle. By the river.

Jane: Hmm. Oh, wait. Yeah, I remember that. Well, you got me there.

Justin: I got it?

Jane: No.

Justin: Oh.

Jane: Yes, I did add the chipmunk on the spur of the moment, and I think I did that while you were feeding Spot that one time. But that's not the thing I was talking about. The thing I hid in the painting is more special than that.

Justin: And you won't tell me what it is?

Jane: What do *you* think?

Justin: I think you won't tell me.

Jane: Bingo.

Justin: *(Heavy sigh)* All right. I'll keep looking.

Jane: Okay. And come over soon for some brownies, okay?

Justin: I will. Bye.

Jane: Bye, Justin.

Needles

The ultrasound stuff
is not working. So today is something new.
Dr. Kim sends me to an elderly doctor
with no hair. I lie on a table
while he slides needles into my arm.
Not just my half-arm, either.
Both arms. And legs.
And a few in my face as well.
It doesn't hurt as much as I feared.
I resemble a porcupine, lying there,
rows of needles
shining under the lights.

Afterward Mom drives me home.
"I hope this helps," she says.
"Me, too." I gaze out the window
at the dry brown mountains rolling past.
I think about the chain of events that
led me to this place.

One trip to the beach.
That was all it took.

Who'd have thought?

Prom Night

Josh: Handsome in his tux.
Brings a corsage that is pale white, fragile;
the petals quiver when he pins it to me.

Limo: Shiny black, reflects streetlights
like winking stars, deep, lush.
Inside, it is crowded, hot, filled with the laughter
of my closest friends.

The gymnasium: Unrecognizable
as a place normally filled with sweat and shouting.
Sparkling lights, red, white, blue, green, and pink;
banners, streamers, wooden tables and chairs;
a band plays on a stage on one end.
Food lines linen-covered tables; the scent of roast beef
and garlic fills the air, mingling with
music and noise.

The dance: Fast, fun, lively, and wild.
Josh laughs, spins; we shake and jump
and laugh the night away.
Whenever a slow song plays,
we sit down, catch our breath, drink something cold.
We watch the couples on the floor
hold each other, as if for dear life,
slowly twirling in small circles.

I prefer the music to be fast and loud.
I prefer to dance and laugh.
Because when things get quiet, and I sit to rest,
I think about the pool,
about Max,
about running away,
about how foolish I felt,
how out of control.

And in bed that night,
my dress slung over the back of my chair,
I echo inside with the *beat-beat* throb of the band,
I recall the heat of the crowd on the dance floor,
I lay my hand on the wilted corsage,
and I focus on all the fun we had.
However . . .
the memory that crowds everything out?

The memory
of running away
from all that
water.

Going for Coffee

"I don't know what's bugging you,
but *something* is,"
Rachel says three days later.

My best friend.
Why do I think I can hide
these things from her?

"Is it your mom?"
she asks. "Has she been
'working late' again?
Mentioned a boyfriend?"

I shake my head.
"No, that's not it."
She pounces.
Figuratively, of course,
because at the moment,
we are walking
down a cracked sidewalk
in town, heading for the coffee shop.
"So there *is* something wrong."

I want to tell her about Max.
About the fiasco at the pool.
"I'll tell you when we get our coffees,"
I say, glancing around.

"I don't want to talk about it
right here."

She leans into me for a second.
"Jane, I'm going to miss you so much
when we go to college."

My stomach lurches
at the reality of being separated
from Rachel.
Before I can respond,
the front door
to the hardware store beside us
swings open
and out walks Max.

Now I Know

Max stops abruptly.
"Hi," he says.
It is then I notice
a large, scruffy man behind him.
The man glowers at Max's back
through shaggy white eyebrows.
He pokes Max in the shoulder.
"And another thing," he says loudly,
angrily. "They know full well
there aren't one hundred screws in the box.
They *know* it. They gouge us that way.
It's because of the microchips in their heads.
They're *trained* to gouge us.
And you just *let* them?"
He throws his hands up in the air.
"You're just like your mother.
Totally useless!"

He stalks off. I stare after him,
dumbfounded,
and after a moment
I swivel my head
back to Max.
His face is bright red.
"Sorry," he says.
He starts to say something else,

then brushes between us
and runs up the sidewalk. "Dad!"

We turn and watch him,
and see him snatch his father's arm
just as the man is about to step off the curb
in front of an oncoming car.

The car slows
and blares its horn.
Max tugs at his father,
who jerks his arm away
and shouts a torrent of anger.
Then they both climb into
Max's old car.

"That's his *dad*?" Rachel asks.
We watch them get into the car,
the father gesticulating the whole time
as Max carefully buckles the seat belt
around his dad's body.
"I guess so," I answer,
aching over what Max is going through.
He doesn't deserve that kind of abuse.
And he lives with it every day?
Aren't there . . . services or agencies? Something?

I picture
what the last three years must have been like

for Max, the three years
since the day his mother died,
leaving him this burden to bear
all alone.
And suddenly I think I get it.
Why Max is studying psychology.
*"It's a great way to help people with their lives.
People who really need it. You know?"*

Yes, Max. I do know.

Now I know.

MENU

Drinks:

Iced Latte (vanilla, caramel, mocha, white chocolate)

Blended Frappe (vanilla, caramel, mocha, white chocolate)

Hot shame and confusion over running away from the pool in front of Max

Assorted Questions over how exactly Max manages a life with all *that*

Gratitude that Mom is healthy and that *she* takes care of *me*

What am I going to do about the pool?

Snacks:

Cake (lemon, gingerbread, coconut, angel food)

Scones (chocolate-chip, cranberry, blueberry)

Crumbling self-esteem

Did you really run away from the pool, Jane?

Rising anxiety: *Could you even make a living as an artist? Really?*

Biscotti (plain, chocolate)

A need to take hold

Cake pops (vanilla, chocolate)

Coffee with Rachel and a talk

A much-needed talk

Doing

When we find our table in the corner,
I sit across from Rachel
and tell her about the swimming pool.
"Wow," Rachel says
when I finish. "Just . . . wow."
We stare at the scone
on the plate between us.
"Why didn't you tell me?" Rachel asks.
"I don't know" is all I can say,
because that's the truth.
After another minute, Rachel says,
"Maybe this is just how it's going to be for you.
Being afraid of water.
Maybe that's how it will always be."

The word *always* hangs in the air,
almost visible
in black, leering letters.
Always afraid? Me?

"I'm sure Max understands," Rachel adds.
I sip and think.
Obviously, Max has things on his mind,
the least of which is me.

The mortification
over how I behaved at the pool

begins to melt away.
In its place is a new focus.

Am I going to be afraid of water the rest of my life?
And if so, am I going to just allow it to be that way?
Is that what I want for myself?

This thing about being disabled.
It's both true, and it's not true.
And in some ways,
it's beginning
to define me.
I'm either working around it,
raging against it,
or wondering about it.
"What should I do?" I ask Rachel.

She sips her latte thoughtfully.
Finally she responds.
"Who says you have to *do* anything?"

I think about this.
Then I disagree.
Doing
or not doing?
That's what defines us.

And right now
I feel as though

I have to reclaim myself.
I don't know *how*
to do that
or what
I mean, exactly.

I just know
it's something
I must
do.

A Paddle

The book I'm reading, *True Stories of Nursing,*
mentions a nurse confined to a wheelchair.
According to this story,
the woman had a reputation
for being hostile and edgy
and so fixated on showing that she could do anything
anyone else could do
that she lost sight of taking care of her patients
and became focused on proving herself.

"Sometimes she was so busy showing off,"
one co-worker wrote,
"that she would do things
that were not in the patient's best interest.
I guess she thought she was a hero
if she did certain big, grand things.
But she was so angry all the time.
The way she behaved ended up
defining her as a person.
And it cost her her job."

I put the book down
and pull up a chair to my art table.
I take out the sketch of Max
and continue shading the depths of his curls,
the thickness of his hair.

Interesting that the book used the word *define*.
That's just what I've been thinking about.
This business of defining
who you are
and *what* you are
and where you are headed —
it's all harder than I thought it would be.
I thought that this stuff
just . . .
happened,
I thought that life
just *happened,*
and I guess I thought
I'd drift right along,
like a leaf on a river,
flowing with the current
to wherever the river wanted to go.

I push the drawing of Max aside,
take up white paper,
and stroke the curve of a leaf,
the stem, the delicate veins.
For so long I've been stuck, confused.
I've been waiting for a sign.
I was "spared" for a reason, some say.
I have a "purpose," some say.

I've been waiting, I guess,
for that reason
and that purpose
to be made clear to me.
I've been drifting. Floating.

Now I see that I have a paddle.
Myself. I'm my own paddle.
I don't have to drift.

Defining who I am
and what I want
and how I'll get there?
It will involve parting
from the current.

It will mean choosing a direction

and beginning
to
paddle.

Letter from Rita
Malibu, California

Dear Jane,

I've been thinking about you for months, ever since I read an update about you. This may sound crazy, but I wanted you to know that your story has changed my life. I look at what happened to you and realize that I have so much to be grateful for, so much I take for granted. I know we are supposed to appreciate our health, but I have to confess I haven't always done so. I am fifty-four years old and have terrible asthma, as well as diabetes and frequent migraines. I can't always do the things I want to do. But you know what? I am alive. And imagining what it would be like to go through life with only one hand has really made me thankful that I don't have to. Seeing you lose so much but pick up and go on with your life, and even give back to others by volunteering at the hospital, makes me ashamed of my past griping and all the excuses I've made. I am embracing what I have, and taking better care of myself, too. For that, I thank you.

I wish you the very best in your young life, and a long and healthy future.

Rita

More

More needles
as I lie on the table
at the acupuncturist.
More heating pads
and ice packs. More time.
More pain.
No results.
I'm playing a game,
trying to outsmart the neuroma,
and it's not working.

Talk

As seven o'clock approaches,
I find myself pacing.
If I had two hands,
I think I'd wring them.
"Everything okay?" Mom asks.
"Everything's fine," I tell her,
then the doorbell rings
and I hurry to answer it.

Max walks in. He looks at me a bit sideways.
Mom chats away. "Jane's science grades
have certainly improved since you started
working together."
Max says, "Well, she's a quick learner."
Mom beams. "She is. When she was five —"

"Mom?" I interrupt desperately.
*We really don't need the
Jane learns to ride a bike story
right now.* "We have to get started.
We have a lot to cover tonight."
"Well, I'll be right here if you need me."
There is a bit of unnecessary emphasis
on *right here.* At last, she's gone.

A tangle of words races through my mind.
The swimming pool incident. The dad incident.

I have mentally rehearsed
addressing these issues
twenty times today.
Why am I frozen now?
How do I even begin?

Then Max clears his throat.
"Jane? We need to talk."

Apologies

I pick up a plate and offer it to him. "Cookie?"
Max shakes his head. "No. We need to—"
He breaks off, and his eyes sharpen.
"Are those oatmeal? Man.
I was *hoping* you'd make those again."
He grabs two cookies. I join him.
We eat in friendly silence. When we're done,
Max gets serious again. "So. Let's talk."

I take a deep breath.
"I'm sorry I ran out on you at the pool.
I'm sure you wondered what was wrong."
He shakes his head. "I did—then you said—
I'm sorry it freaked you out like that."
He folds his hands.
"But I'm glad about something, too."
I trace a crack on the tabletop. "Oh?"
He suddenly puts a hand over mine.
"I'm glad you tried."

My stomach flips.
"It was courageous," Max adds.
An ugly snort escapes my lips.
"Hardly," I mutter,
pulling my hand away.
Is he just being nice?
Because surely he doesn't mean it.

"Hey," Max says, and he sounds stern.
"Stop it. I'm not just *saying* that.
I *mean* it. I don't say things I don't mean."

I try to believe him.
"Facing the water again
was *courageous,*" Max repeats.
"So you weren't ready. So what?
The important thing is
you made that first step.
Next time, it will be easier."

His words sound so confident and simple.
And they conjure up the time
Rachel and I went out for coffee
just after I'd lost my arm.
It was so hard.
But we did it.
Together, we did it.
And I told myself then
that the next time would be easier.
And the next time, and the next.
So . . . could Max be right?

Is there even going to be *a next time?*

"That's up to you," he says.
I jump, then realize in dismay
that I said the words out loud.

I clear my throat.
"I don't know. I just . . .
I'm not sure. It was pretty . . . awful . . .
when I saw all that . . . water."
Well said, Jane. Well said.

He nods as though what I'm saying
is not disjointed and stupid.
Maybe because he's used to living with
a crazy person
who says crazy things.
Jane, what an awful thought.
"Anyway. I apologize for freaking out on you."

"No problem. But I have a question.
I guess I already know the answer, but —
have you been back to the beach
since the accident?"

I shake my head again.
"No. I've thought about it.
A lot of times. I always thought I would.
Just — just because.
I figured I'd go back there
and prove to myself I was fine
and that it was all over
and I can live a normal life
and go to the beach if I want.
But after what happened at the pool,

I'm not ready for that."
I swallow. "I'm not sure if I ever will be."

I am shocked
hearing myself say this.
Until just now,
I guess I didn't know
I felt that way.
I guess I believed I could handle
anything that came my way.

Guess I was wrong.
And maybe this fear
will define parts of me, after all.

So much
for taking up an oar
and paddling.

Max's Turn

We sit for a moment,
deep in our own thoughts.
Then I jump in with the next thing.
"About running into you in town . . ."

Max sighs miserably. "About that.
I am sorry my dad was being a . . .
well, a lunatic. He gets like that sometimes."
"It's okay," I tell him. "I'm just sorry that . . ."
I break off as he gives me a sharp frown.
That you have to live *with him*
is what I'd been about to say.
Good grief, Jane. You can't say that.
"I'm sorry about everything."

"My dad has been mentally ill a long time,
but we had it under control," Max says.
"It was okay. Over the last few years,
he's started slipping.
He won't take his medicine sometimes.
He gets worked up and angry. And when he does . . .
he's not himself." He shrugs, dejected.
"He's going to have to go to a home soon.
I just can't bear to do that to him."

Sitting there at the table,
Max, despite his broad shoulders

and strong swimmer's arms,
looks so much like a small, helpless boy
that I almost reach out and hug him.
"Is that why you live at home
and went to school here in town?"
I ask him gently.
He looks at me sharply again.
"Yeah, it is. I guess pretty much everyone
knows that I passed up scholarships
to better schools." He pauses.
"That was *my* choice. I *wanted* to stay with Dad.
I did it for me as much as for him.
So you don't have to look at me like that."

"Like what?"

"Like you're sorry for me.
Don't, okay?"
He sounds annoyed now.
Mortified, I stare at my fingers.
I am *sorry for you,*
I want to say. *How could I not be?*
Then I think about what he said.
Haven't I thought the same thing
a million times?
I wonder, does Max feel sorry for *me?*
I don't want that from him. From *anyone.*
And here I sit, feeling sorry for Max
when he doesn't want me to.

"Okay. I won't," I say.
And though it might not happen overnight,
I *will* try. Max doesn't need my pity.
He needs a friend.

Max nods. "Good."
He clears his throat.
"And now I have one more question for you."
I take out my pen and get ready to work.
"Yes?"

He folds his arms and leans on the table.
He is close to me.
Very close.
"Do you have a boyfriend?"

Asking

The room grows small
and still as I answer, "No."
We sit a minute.
"Do you have a girlfriend?" I ask.
He shakes his head.
"You'd be surprised how many girls
are not interested in a guy
who still lives at home
and has no money
and drives a beat-up car
and can't have anyone over
because his dad will go ballistic."

"What about Brittany?
And Sarah?" I ask.
He frowns, scratching his chin.
"Brittany? She's my cousin.
She's a retired nurse.
She lives nearby and takes care of Dad
when I can't be at home.
And Sarah is just a friend.
She's dating a guy I'm friends with.
How did you even . . . ?"
He trails off. "*Oh*. The day we met.
At the cafeteria? With the tutor?"

"Yes. I thought . . ."

He sighs. "No. She's not.
And here I thought . . . well.
I'm still friends with guys at the high school.
They mentioned seeing you at prom.
With a guy."

Josh.

"Josh is just a friend," I tell him quickly.
"He already has a girlfriend, but she couldn't go to prom."
Oh, dear. Here he thought . . .
and I thought . . .
"I am not dating anyone," I say.

"Me, either," Max says.
We stare at each other,
the silence loud in the room.
I think, for the first time,
I am seeing Max as a person.
Not as *Max* the dazzling swim star
or *Max* the person I made him up to be.

I see him as a guy — not much older than me —
working his way through college,
doing the best he can
with what he's got
and what he's lost.

He lost his mother,
he gained the full-time care of his father,
he's good at math, he loves to laugh,
he likes to read, he's a good listener,
and he wants to be a psychologist.
He's patient and smart.
And right now,
he looks at me in a way
that makes me question
everything I ever thought I knew
about boys
and love
and life.

"I want to know if you'll do something for me,"
Max asks.
My mouth goes dry. "What is it?"
"I want you to come back to the pool,"
Max says. "One more time.
Come early on Saturday.
Before it's open to everyone else.
It will be just you and me.
Promise."

Schools of small fish flip their tails
inside my stomach. "What for?"
"Because you can do this," Max says.
He places his hand over mine.
"And because I'm asking.

I'm asking you on a date, Jane.
Will you come?"

Would I be the first girl in the universe
to do something crazy
for a boy just because he asks?
Probably not.
But . . . do I *want* to go?
Back to *that*?
To the shame? The terror?
And all that *water*?

Looking into Max's eyes,
I'm shocked to discover:
the answer is
yes.

Food for Thought

And then I tell Max
something I haven't told anyone.
Not even, really, myself.
"I don't want to be a nurse anymore."

There.
I said it. And the universe
does not react,
does not scream;
there are no lightning bolts
or earthquakes,
no wails of agony.
I do not
shatter into a thousand shards.
In fact, Max
does not even let go of my hand.
He thinks a moment.
"What *do* you want to do?" he asks.

"Art." As soon as I say it,
tears spring to my eyes.
"I want to be an artist,
just like I always wanted to be.
I thought I wanted to be a nurse.
And I like helping at the hospital.
But I don't want to do that forever.
I want to be an artist. *Forever.*"

Max squeezes my hand.

"Then why don't you do that?"

"Because I went and told everyone
that maybe I wanted to be a nurse.
And everyone got excited. And I feel
like I *have* to follow through.
Like I'm letting people down if I . . .
I mean, it would be so selfish if I . . ."

Max interrupts. "Slow down. First of all,
who would you be letting down?"

*The billions of people who write to me and tell me I'm
inspirational. The people who are hurt,
who need someone who's been there.
The people who saved my life.
Lindsey. Doctors. Everyone. That's who.*
But my throat tightens, and I can't even speak.

"I'd think your family would want you
to be happy, and to do art, if that's what you want,"
Max says. "It's not like it's out of the blue.
You said this is something you've always wanted.
So who would you disappoint?"

"I'm not sure" is all I can think to say.

"When I was in the hospital . . . everyone helped. . . .

It was so good to be helped . . . and I thought . . .”
Great. I can't finish a single sentence.
“I thought I could do the same. I thought I could help.
I thought maybe, in a way, I was *meant* to change paths.”

“You thought that? Or did everyone *tell* you that?”

I glance at him.
He cocks his head. “Do you think you *need* to be a nurse
in order to prove something?
Or to satisfy something? Guilt, maybe?”

Wow. That psychology training really works.
As I fumble for a response, Max says,
“Is that a good reason to go into medicine?
Because everyone *else* wants you to?
Because you think you *should*?”

His words sink in slowly, like melted lead
filling up the cracks and pores in my insides.
The people in the hospital I see every Saturday —
they are real people, not plastic dummies or volunteers
or stories or characters. *Real. People.*

With real injuries. Real illness
and heartaches and real families.
Can I devote myself to their care if,
for even one second,

my heart lies somewhere else?
"I never thought of it that way."

Max squeezes my hand again.
"You should."
We lock eyes, and for one moment,
I think I may actually kiss him,
and then Mom calls from the hallway,
"How about some popcorn?"
We barely manage to drop hands and pull apart
before she turns the corner and asks,
"Anyone want anything?"
"No, thanks, Mom." I sigh.
Max stands. "I was just leaving."
I say nothing as he puts on his coat
and nods good-bye to us both.
But, oh. The words we have spoken.
They hang in the air, so ripe I could pick them,
could take a bite and savor them.

And for the rest of the night,
that is exactly what I do.

5. Win the School Art Competition

Justin takes my hand as we walk into the makeshift
gallery, already filled with students and parents,
wandering the aisles, poring over the art.
"Yours is going to *win*," he whispers.
That's what I like about Justin.
Without seeing the other pieces,
he *knows* I'm the best. Friends like him
don't come along every day.

I squeeze his hand back. "I hope so."
Michael, who has come home for the weekend
and who drove us here, pokes me in the shoulder.
"Do they have a snack booth here? A bake sale?
Candy?"
I turn and give him what I hope is a withering stare.
"It's an art show, Michael. Not a fruit stand."
He holds up his hands. "Touchy, touchy.
Fine. We'll look at art. But it wouldn't kill anyone
to have some food here. That's all I'm saying."

There is the usual mix of media.
Pastels, oils, acrylic, chalk, charcoal,
pencil, watercolor, pen and ink.
Subjects range from animals to landscapes,
houses, farms, and portraits.
Elizabeth and Rachel find us.
"Let's go find your painting," Rachel says.

My *Skies and Seas* painting hangs by the doorway,
on a wall with other landscapes. One next to mine
catches my eye—a street scene, in the rain, at dusk.
Moody, shadowy, and well lit, it's beautiful.

Mrs. Foxe steps up onto the stage.
"Thank you for coming, and congratulations to *all* our
artists,"
she says, beaming around the room as everyone gathers.
"I know I say this every year, but honestly—
this is the *best show yet*."
Justin nudges me. He asks in a whisper,
"Does she really say that every year?"
I nod. "She does."

"And now for our winners," Mrs. Foxe says,
unfolding a piece of paper. "The judges
wanted me to tell you all that they had a *very*
hard time choosing this year, because everything
was just so wonderful."
She announces the winners
for pastels, then watercolors, then charcoal.
Then she reaches my category. Acrylics.

"And for first prize in acrylics, the ribbon goes to . . .
Josh Macintosh."

Shock

Josh? As in . . . my prom date, Josh?
He emerges from the crowd, grinning,
towing along a pretty girl.
He takes the blue ribbon from Mrs. Foxe,
with the same hand that pinned the corsage
to my dress on prom night. Well.
Didn't see that coming.

As applause spatters from the crowd,
I experience rude shock, confusion, and paralysis.
I did not win.
My hard work, my beautiful piece —
one of the very few *true* pieces
I have to show for myself since the accident —
it *did not win.*
And I was so sure it would.
Until now, I guess I didn't realize
how much I assumed I would *win.*

How arrogant can you get?
The sense of loss I have?
It comes from feeling
entitled.
And in art,
you are *not ever* entitled.
I know that. And I know
that judging art is so subjective.

It's one of the worst things you can do to art,
actually — judge it and place a ribbon on it.

But that's what I counted on here today.
Winning.
Good idea or not, in the past, when I won those ribbons,
they meant everything. They brought joy and pride.
And they told me that I was the best
at *something.*

And the crystal-clear reality?
I thought I deserved that ribbon,
more than anyone, this year of years.
After all, didn't I work hard?
Didn't I come so far?

Didn't I?

Red

"Second prize goes to Jane Arrowood."
It takes Michael giving me a sharp poke
to bring me back to the moment.
"Congratulations, Jane." Mrs. Foxe
holds out a shiny red ribbon.
I propel myself toward her and
take the ribbon while everyone in the room
applauds wildly. Loudly.

Rachel leans forward as I join her.
"Jane, look." She gestures behind me.
I turn around, and the crowd
has edged forward in a mass,
and they are still clapping. Mr. Musker
is at the front.

Someone whistles, piercing and shrill.
Someone says, "Good for you, Jane!"
Someone else yells, "Way to go, Jane!"
And in the ensuing long, long round of clapping,
in which even Michael joins in,
everyone cheers.
For me.

6. Qualify for and Enter the West Coast Wings Art Competition
7. Win the West Coast Wings Art Competition

I'm still glowing, still smiling, still crazy
out of sync with my heartbeat,
which has skyrocketed off to the heavens
somewhere. Even now, as we walk to the exit,
parents give me a thumbs-up, a heartfelt
"So good to see you painting again, Jane.
We missed you last year.
Keep going, Jane. You're amazing."

Justin takes my hand once more.
"That was *awesome*.
I hope someday people clap for *me*
that way."
I squeeze his hand. "Something tells me
they will."

Before we leave, we seek out Josh
and his girlfriend. He lights up when he sees us.
"Hi, guys. This is Kathy, my girlfriend from back
home."
We all say hello. Kathy seems shy.
"Congratulations," I tell Josh,
and everyone chimes in, too.
"I didn't know you painted,"

I say. And the truth?
I didn't know because I never asked.

When I talked to Max about nursing,
I reflected on the people in the hospital
and how their real needs, their real lives,
are not stories or toys to be played with.
They're *real.*
I never applied that reasoning to Josh.
Since prom, have I made one iota of an effort
to find him in the halls? Say hello? Like I *said* I would?
Nope. And that selfish attitude?
It's going to stop.
Right now.

"Your painting is gorgeous," I tell him.
He grins. "Thanks." He points toward the display.
"So is yours. Wow. And that round of applause
for you? *Wow.*"
"Yeah, that was a . . . surprise."

Mr. Musker joins us and puts an arm
around both of us. "There's my two champs.
Congratulations, both of you. I'm so proud,
and you should be, too."
"I am," Josh says.
I agree. "Me, too."
And now that I've had a moment to think it over?

I *am*.
That blue ribbon? It means a lot.
The cheers and support of the entire crowd?
That means even more.

When I go to bed that night,
I take out my bucket list.
I won't accomplish numbers
five, six, and seven.
But I did gain something.
Something more valuable
than first place.
Perspective.
You can't put a price on that.

However.
Sliding into bed, I have to laugh at myself.
The reality? The *humble* reality?
I wouldn't have minded gaining perspective

and

a blue ribbon
at the same time.

Holding Hands

"I'm seeing someone."
Mom blurts this out the instant
she walks into the kitchen.
I set down the tray of scones
I've pulled from the oven.
"And good morning to you, too, Mom."

She laughs in a shaky way,
then sits down at the table.
"Sorry. I had to get it out
before I lost my nerve again."
She sits back and folds her arms.
"You're not surprised," she declares.
"How long have you known?"
I turn back to the scones,
biting my lip. "Um. A while?"

"I guess all that working late stuff
gave it away, huh?" she continues,
and with a whoosh of gratitude, I nod.
Mom watches me sit down.
We bask in the scent of cinnamon before
Mom puts a scone on her plate.
"His name is Rich," she says.

I select a scone, too.
"I like a man with an adjective for a name."

She sips her coffee. "You're taking this
better than I imagined."
"What did you imagine?" I ask.
"Oh . . . panic.
Indignation. Twenty questions."
If she only knew.
"What does he do?"
I hold out my cup as she pours us both juice.
"He's a veterinarian, actually," Mom says.
"From Pasadena. I want you to meet him."

A veterinarian? A healer, then.
Maybe this guy is good enough for Mom.
I sure hope so.
"Tell me about him," I say.
Mom beams like Cupid got her.
I have so many questions,
yet I ask none of them.
All these months of wondering,
and waiting, and worrying
about what Mom is doing
and if she's going to get married
and if my world will turn upside down?
They boil down to this:

fresh scones,
the tick of the clock,

Mabel's small sticky yawn,
and my mom across the table from me.
A moment of peace
before a hectic day at school.

All of this is going to change
in a few short months.
Not because of a boyfriend.
Not even because of a potential stepfather.
But because.

Because of time
and growing up and moving on
and going to college and building a life
and drawing and painting
and helping and healing
and friends who stay friends
even when time is scarce
and distance is great.

All this time
we've had our oars in the water,
all of us, and we've been busily paddling
on our own individual little paths.
I never really saw it till now.
And the thing that I suddenly see
that keeps me calm?

The realization that
as much as we've been paddling,
we've all managed
to hold on to each other.
No matter what the storms,
we've held on to each other.

Rachel and I will travel our separate paths.
But we'll always be Jane and Rachel.
Justin will be Justin, and I will never let him go.
My home, my world, my *comfort zone,*
as Rachel says? It's not a place.
It's not a frozen moment in time.
It's inside,
in my heart,
full of the pieces of everyone
I love.

Things will change.
But love won't.

9. Bake a Wedding Cake

"If you get married,"
I say to Mom
as we put away our dishes,
"I have one request."

"What is it?" she asks warily.

"I want to bake the wedding cake."

She pulls me into a hug.
"It's a deal."
Then she kisses me
on the top of the head,
like I'm a small toddler.
"I love you," she says.

"I love you, too, Mom."

Letter from Quinn
San Clemente, California

Dear Jane,

I saw a follow-up story about you in a magazine. I'm so glad to hear that you are well and that you are back in school. I always wondered what happened to you.

Jane — you are a huge *inspiration to me. I'm an artist, like you. And there was a time in my life when I really struggled with it, with finding my own style, with mastering some of the techniques I wanted to, and with finding acceptance from my family. They like my art. They just don't like the idea of me doing it for a living.*

When I read your follow-up story and found out you were back in school and getting ready to graduate, I said to myself, "If that girl can lose her entire drawing arm and still keep working at the things she cares about and still keep going with her life without giving up or breaking down, then who am I to complain about anything?"

You've given me a fresh perspective, and for that, I thank you. I also wish you the best, as one girl to another, one artist to another, one person to another. Best wishes for a long and happy future.

Your friend,
Quinn

Truth

"See you Sunday," Rachel says
as we walk to our separate buses.

"See you then."

She pauses.
"Have any plans for tomorrow?"

I think of my date with Max.
At the pool. Which could very well
turn into an even bigger disaster
than last time.
I don't want to talk about it.
Yet. So I only say,
"Yeah, I do, actually.
I'll tell you about it later."

She cocks her head, eyes burning with curiosity.
Anyone else would give me the third degree right now.

But Rachel is not anyone else.
She is Rachel.
And she only says,
"You better."

The Pool . . . Again

Saturday morning.
The whole world is dark
and still.

I tiptoe from the house and
ride my bike to the school.
Lights are on in the pool house.
My flip-flops slap
across the pavement.
Not even the birds are cheeping this early.

Easing open the giant door,
I see Max, already in the water.
He's swimming.
Cleanly, quietly, cutting through the water
with strong, smooth strokes.
Water slips around him, over him,
like liquid air.

He reaches the end of the lane,
pops up, and removes his goggles,
breathing heavily.
Then he turns and sees me.
A smile lights his face,
and in response,
as if my feet no
longer belong to my body,

I find myself
walking
toward the pool,
toward the water,

toward him.

Courage

I stop a few feet away.
Max glides closer.
When he reaches the edge,
we stare at each other, our smiles gone.
I take off my wrap and let it fall.

I have never felt so naked,
standing there in my bathing suit,
with my half-arm,
my body, and all my terror exposed.
I can do nothing
but listen to myself breathe.

It's no different this time.
The sight of so much water,
flickering under the lights —
undulating, rocking, in the area around Max,
the smell of chlorine and the sound
of lapping, quiet lapping,
against the edges of the pool,
the small whoosh of water as Max
moves effortlessly
to the edge of the pool —
all of it combines to induce paralysis.
I tremble, even though I'm not cold.
I am aware of Max, climbing the ladder,

walking over to me, dripping a trail of wet
across the floor.

I pull my gaze from the pool,
and there in Max's magnetic eyes,
so dark and patient,
I find something. Comfort.
Courage.

The Edge

Max takes my hand and
leads me to the edge.
Sitting down, he puts his feet in the water.
He pats the ground next to him.
Shivering, I sit next to him.
I sit on his right side, so that my half-arm
is away from him, and hug my knees with my left arm.

I remember when I used to swim,
when I would float or dive under,
how the pressure of water in my ears
would create a profound silence.
I used to like that.
Shutting off the world that way.

And I remember the sound from that day.
Or at least, I think I remember,
though doctors tell me I can't —
I remember the roar of water rushing,
gushing, into my ears, into my mouth,
down my throat. I remember shouts and cries.
I shiver harder; my stomach clenches.
"Maybe this wasn't such a good idea."
Max waits, then nods his wet head.
"Maybe I'm not ready," I go on.
"Maybe I should leave."
He squeezes my hand. "Okay."

We sit there a minute longer,
the water lapping, lapping, against its constraints.
"So . . ." I say, to fill the silence.
"Is this . . . therapy?
Psychology stuff from your classes?
What would you call this, exactly?"
He gazes down at his feet in the water.
"Hmm. Tell you what.
Let's call it . . . immersion therapy."

We look at each other, at the space
between our faces where smiles should be.
I run a finger along the pebbly, rough concrete.
Max's legs are stuck out over the side,
strong legs, tapering into nothingness in the water,
his feet melted from view. He puts his hand over mine.
He waits for me to decide if I'm going to do this or not.

All I have to do is get up
and go back to the locker room
and change. Change myself
into clothes,
instead of someone who's brave
and can face her fears.
That's all I need to do.

But I don't want to be that person.
I don't want to be the girl—

Shark Girl—
who can't face a swimming pool.

I close my eyes
and focus all my being
on the touch, the weight, of Max's hand.
It's an anchor.
It's a rock.

Then, before I can back out,
I shift
and thrust my feet
into the water
one
by
one.

Dive

The water is cold;
my skin tingles in tiny pops.
I let out my breath,
shaky and quick.

Then I look at Max,
so steady and calm.
He watches,
waiting for the next cue.

I hear myself say,
"I'm ready."
And in one motion, one fluid motion,
at the exact same moment,
as though we had rehearsed this,
as though we both knew exactly what came next,
we slide our bodies off the edge
and   into   the   water.

Float

Cool water engulfs me.
My legs kick too hard, and for a minute
I'm all splash and flounder and choke and flail.
The horrible, empty chasm
beneath my body — it's frightening.
Plenty of room in the water
for a huge fish
with a gaping mouth
to swim up beneath me,
to bite,
to pull down and sever.
"Max," I gasp, kicking helplessly.

"It's all right." Directly in my ear,
softly, so softly that I have to pause to hear him.
In that pause, he threads his hands
beneath my underarms.
Below us,
his legs tread, tread water,
supporting us both.
"I've got you."

I take a slow breath,
the first rule in any panicky situation.
I take another. And another.
Something in my chest unknots a little.

Max tilts, then glides backward,
towing me along on top of him,
his chin in my hair, his hands on my shoulders.
I gaze up at the ceiling.
Slowly we move through the water.
"Rest your legs," he murmurs in my ear.

I have to close my eyes and concentrate
to still my panicked legs.
My head comes to rest on his collarbone.
Our wet bodies, soaking hair, merge.
"Jane," he says again. "Relax. Trust me."

There is no danger here, Jane. None.
I focus on softening every inch of my body,
shutting down all defenses,
all tense places, all images
and worries, one by one.

"Good," Max breathes into my ear,
his chin scraping the side of my face.
His breath is warm on my neck.
A wave of heat washes over me.
"Just go along for the ride," he murmurs.

The water parts for us
with barely a ripple.
As we move about the pool,
side to side, and side to side,

I melt into Max's body
a little more, then a little more,
until Max and I are a single mermaid,
a soft rope, twined around and around,
a scrap of a jellyfish, moving weightlessly
on a current.
I relax my neck the last little bit,
and my ears slide under the water.

Whoosh.
The silence I remember
fills my ears.
Shutting off the world.

I come up for air, soft and safe in Max's arms.
The truth of this moment?
This moment, that I dreaded so?

I don't want it to end.

Friends

Justin calls me that night.
"I found it!" he crows.
"Found what?" I ask, feigning confusion.
Triumph rings from his voice.
"I found the thing you hid in the mural.
It's us, isn't it? It's you and me,
and we're walking together."
I let out a dramatic sigh.
"You win. That's it."
He laughs. "We're so tiny,"
he says, and I can tell he's looking
at the painting right now.
"I barely found us, walking in the middle
of all the other people."

I picture the miniature people we painted,
strolling up and down that path.
Moms pushing strollers. Kids walking dogs.
Dads holding hands with their daughters.
And me and Justin, two friends side by side,
fingertips touching.
"I'm holding a LEGO monster in one hand,"
Justin says, giggling.

"I know how much you like LEGOs,"
I tell him, thinking back to the many sessions
of LEGO building we've done together.

"I like it," Justin says. "I like it that we're in it."

"Me, too," I tell him. And I do.

Inside that mural that we worked so long over,

in one frozen moment,

Justin and I,

we will forever be next to each other.

No matter where I go, no matter where *he* goes,

no matter what happens,

in that single patch of painting,

Justin and I will always be in the same place,

at the same time.

Two friends.

Two kids.

Holding on.

Some Things

After saying good night to Justin,
I put on my pajamas and find a book to read.
But as I climb into bed,
my arm begins to throb painfully.
I hold it awhile, wishing the pain away.

If only life were as easy as making a painting.
Where you could control
the outcome, dictate the weather, erase
your mistakes, and paint over the big questions.
If only we could paint big sunflowers
over our pain. Over our heart's turmoil.

But then again, maybe not.
Turmoil is what brought Justin
into my life in the first place.
Besides, some things are meant to last forever.
Like friendship. And good feelings.

And some things are meant to be dealt with,
head-on.
No matter how hard it is.

Navigating

"The alternative therapies
are not working,"
Dr. Kim says, reviewing my file.

As though I don't know this.
As though right now, I am not sitting
in a pool of discomfort, my arm buzzing again.
"We could try something new.
Medication, perhaps."

"I want the surgery," I tell him.
Dr. Kim blinks. "You do? I thought you were — er,
hesitant to go that route."
"I was. Not anymore.
What I want is the quickest,
most effective way
to get rid of this pain."
As I say it, I know it's true.
Truer than anything I've said for a long time.

Enough games. This pain is done
nagging at me, burdening me.
If I can cut it from my life,
why wouldn't I?

Mom speaks up. "We've talked this over,
Doctor. Jane is prepared to have the surgery.

Before she begins school in the fall, if possible."
Dr. Kim stuffs his pen into his shirt pocket.
"Good for you, Jane.
Let me get some information,
and we'll go over the specifics.
Then I'll set you up with scheduling."
He pauses by the door. "There are no promises,
of course. But I do think those flare-ups
will be greatly reduced."

No promises.
Do all doctors have to say that?
I guess they do.
And really?
Life should come with such a statement.
No promises.
Just lots of hope.
"I know," I tell him.
"I'm ready."

Better

Rachel and I sit out on the back steps,
iced teas and cupcakes nearby.
"School is almost over," Rachel says.
"You ended up with great grades.
Complete with a B in science.
Hmm . . . who can we thank for *that*?"
I grin. "That was the best B I ever earned."
She picks up a cupcake. "Now you have good grades
to show to any of those four schools you end up in."

My smile fades. Since my talk with Max,
about wanting to be an artist,
I've sat with those thoughts
a good long while. They haven't tiptoed away.
In fact, they are stronger than ever.
An artist. That's what I want.

But I haven't had the guts to tell anyone yet.
Not even my best friend.
Instead, I float a question to her, hoping it sounds casual.
"Let's say I choose art school.
I'm a little worried about something."
She sighs. "You worry too much, Jane. What is it?"
"My artwork. It's not where I want it to be yet.
What are the chances I'll do well in art school?
With my work being . . ."

Rachel pushes a strand of hair out of my eyes.
"Fantastic? Jane, remember something.
Your artwork is almost *never* good enough to satisfy you.
You've always felt that way, even *before* the accident.
That's why you're such a good artist. You always
push to do to better. And besides,
isn't that the whole point of art school?
To learn? And get better? You don't go into
something like that *perfect,* right?
As for your chances? I say
you have just as good a chance as anyone."

Not so long ago, I would have laughed bitterly
at such a statement. But now?
She's right. One-handed, that's me.
But I'm surely not the only one-handed person
to ever apply to college, or pick up a pencil,
or help out at a hospital.
I'm surely not the only one-handed person
to ever wander in confusion,
to hope. To dream.

"I'm so happy for you," I tell Rachel.
"Getting into the school you wanted.
San Diego is such a great place.
I'm going to come visit you sometimes."

"You better," Rachel says with a grin.
Her phone beeps and she picks it up

and reads a text.
"Mom's on her way over," she says.
Rachel's mom is taking us
to pick up our caps and gowns.
Graduation is three days away.

"Are you ready?" she asks.
We look at each other.
Am I ready? Is she? Are *we*?
Either way, it's happening.
I reach out to my best friend
and give her a one-armed hug.
She wraps both arms around me
in return. One of us is sniffling.

"Yes," I tell her.
"I'm ready."

Access

"I can't believe tomorrow is our last day
of school," Elizabeth says.
"Do you think Max will come to graduation?"
She sounds hopeful.

"No . . . he has to take his dad somewhere."
Max is making some changes.
He's doing what he has to
to make sure his dad
is cared for. Properly.
Today he finalized paperwork.
This weekend, his dad will move into
assisted living.

I don't mention that although Max will not be here
this weekend, he *is* coming here today.
All day my nerves are high,
due to our private agenda for this afternoon.
When he picks me up at school,
I ask him, "How did it go?"

"Good," he says, though he sounds worn out.
"It's all taken care of, and we're on track
for moving him this weekend.
It's hard. Still. I can't count on Brittany forever.
And I can't be there all day.
It's time to get Dad into a better situation.

Meanwhile, still want to do this?"
I buckle up. "Yes."
The word is tight, clipped.

"You look sick," he says.
"I know this was your idea, but . . ."
"Max." I roll my head sideways toward him.
"You're a psychology major, right?
This is it. This is about closure.
Before I start college.
Before I take one more step
doing *anything*. I need to see if . . .
well. You know."
He starts the car. "Yes," he says. "I know."

"I'm sorry about your dad," I tell him.
He touches the steering wheel.
"Thanks. But . . . it's going to be okay.
If my mom were still here,
I think she'd agree. It's what's best."

After that, there's not much to say.
We drive in silence for an hour
to the small road with the sign that says
BEACH ACCESS.

The Point

I catch a glimpse of sand and a strip
of glittering blue, stretching all along the horizon.
My shoulders go numb, and my breath runs dry.
Max parks in a sandy lot. Overhead,
gulls spin in the sky,
wheeling on a breeze, and I smell the ocean.
Has the sea always smelled that way?
So heavy, so alive? So . . . dangerous?
I should cancel this whole crazy thing.

Then I look at Max.
I remember the pool.
I think about fear
ruling parts of my life
and how I don't want that
anymore. "Ready?" I ask.

"Yes," Max replies.
Together, we step out of the car.
Together, we walk toward the beach.
The same beach
where I lost my arm
to a shark.

On the Beach

So hot, this sand beneath my feet.
So smooth, the sound of air and water,
the way they meet just above the chop,
in that soft, rushing *swish* —
the surf does not "roar," as some say it does.
The ocean whispers in many voices.

So alive, these people, dotted all along the shore.
Children dash to the edge of the lapping, foamy surf,
then race away, shrieking, legs grazed by curls of water.
A dog gallops past, carrying a heavy stick.
Far out in the gray water,
sleek surfers bob on the surface,
corks in a bathtub, straddling their boards.
One pushes his arms into the water.
They do not see how small they are
against an immense horizon.

Heavy on the air is the scent of suntan lotion,
and seagulls cry overhead, floating, always floating,
clouds of white kites, seeking popcorn and crumbs.

All of this, I have seen scores of times.
I have been to this beach
countless afternoons;
even my father brought me here,
when he was alive.

Today
it's a barely remembered dream;
it's a foreign world,
a homeland I have forgotten,
a place where I once lived and breathed and swam
but now find incomprehensible.
I don't know what I expected to feel,
but it's not this.

My stomach lies deathly still.
My body takes in
the warmth of the sun,
the grit of sand.
My mind does not go
to that scary place
it went before.
It does not imagine awful things.
Instead, my mind whispers:
We don't belong here anymore.

I don't. I am a fish out of water here,
and this sinks in, more and more plainly,
as a long, long time passes
with Max and I walking slowly along the shore.
I try to pinpoint the feeling I have right now.
Not relief, and not sadness, either.
Just a quiet acceptance.
Finally, miles from where we started,
I stop and stand. I look out at the horizon.

Lightness steals across my body,
as though a heavy iron chain
curled around my neck has broken
and fallen to the ground.
A chain
I didn't even know I carried
until now.

What did I expect by coming here?
I wasn't sure. But now?
The question has been answered.
Can I face the beach? *Yes.*
Can I stand here and be calm? *Yes.*
Do I *want* to be here?
Do I want to come back, over and over,
like I used to?
Do I want to swim,
to prove something?
Do I *need* to?

No.
I will not swim in that gray mass again,
and I understand without a trace of doubt
that I no longer will feel a need to visit this beach.
Not because I'm afraid. But because
I'm done.

Closure.
Is that what this is?

I am able to look around
and see the beauty of the water.
I do not see the ghost of myself,
lying in tatters on the sand.
For that, I am grateful.
And that, in my book,
is peace.

This place, as lovely as it is,
holds no interest for me anymore.
And no power, either.

"What are you thinking?" Max asks,
and I jump. I have forgotten he is beside me.
I look around once more.
"I think I'm ready to go home."
He gazes out at surfers, paddling away.
"That bad, huh?"

"No. It's not like that. Really."
I turn to him.
My life is just beginning.
And it starts today.
"I'm not upset," I tell Max. "I'm just . . ."

Grateful.
For some reason,
I am reluctant to speak the word out loud.
"I'm not afraid,

but I'm not going back in, either.
I'm just . . . *done*. If that makes sense."

"Yeah, it does, actually." He sizes me up.
"I can see it in your eyes.
Something's changed in there.
You look . . . taller, kind of. Free."

He blushes, and I love him for being the sort of person
who blushes at himself. I surprise myself
by taking his hand.
"That's it exactly. I'm free."

"I'm glad." Max says.
The wind blows my hair all across my face,
but I don't want to let go of Max's hand
long enough to push it away.

Max reaches up and does it for me.
Pushing my hair behind my shoulder,
he tucks it behind my ear,
gently pushes it off my cheeks.

Then
he leans in

and kisses me.

Joy

My very being
lifts
somewhere high above me,
out of my body,
hovers like a hummingbird,
my toes curl in their sandals,
my heart races,
faster and faster
and
f
a
s
t
e
r

and joy fills me

     all   the   way
              to   the
                top.

All Places

Max pulls away from our kiss,
taking my hand in both of his.
He blinks as though surprised.
"Jane. I didn't mean for that to happen. . . .
Not here, anyway.
That's not what today was about.
Of all places to . . . *do* this . . . I . . ."

"Hey, Max?"
I step forward, stand on tiptoe,
and, still clutching his hand,
I put my lips to his
and
kiss him back.

Going Home

Riding home in Max's car,
he holds my left hand in his right one
while he drives.
I watch in the side mirror
as the sparkling ocean dwindles away,
smaller and smaller. We drive on,
wind scattering through our hair.

Fear
no longer rules
any part of my life.
I know now
what it means
to reclaim myself.
And what it means
to kiss Max.

All it took
was one trip to the beach.

Who'd have thought?

Heart

"I've made my decision,"
I tell Mom. "It's art school."
I show her the brochure
for the college I've chosen.
Mom squeals and throws her arms around me.
"I *knew* you'd make the right choice,"
she says in my ear.

"You didn't want me to go to nursing school?"
I ask, confused. "Why didn't you say so?"
Mom holds me at arm's length.
"It's not that I *didn't* want you to go there.
I just wanted you to make the choice
that would make you happiest. All this time
you've been agonizing, you haven't been happy.
But now you are. I can see it in your eyes, honey.
I can see you made the right choice for *you*."
We hug again. I sure wish I'd talked this over with her
earlier. Maybe I wouldn't have struggled so long.
Why do I always think I need to do things alone?
Max's words come back to me:
Your family would want you to do art,
if that's what you want.
So who would you disappoint?

Mom is so steadfast,
and yet full of surprises, too.

Am I surprised she's supportive?
Not really. What I am surprised about?
How well she knows me. And how much
I value her support.

Later, we crunch the numbers, go over
scholarship applications,
and decide that for sure
we can make it work.
We give each other a high-five.

I get on the phone and I tell Rachel my decision.
She cries a little. "I knew it," she says.
"I would have supported you either way,
but I have to admit, I was hoping you'd pick art.
That day on the steps, when we talked . . .
I could tell you'd made your choice but
weren't ready to talk about it. It's been killing me
not saying anything. But, Jane? I am *so glad* for you."

Rachel. So full of surprises. All this time,
and she hasn't pushed her agenda on me.
She's given me the room I needed to think this over,
to make peace with it,
before talking about it.
She's another one
I wouldn't trade for anything,
not even my right arm.

"I love you," I tell her.
"I love you, too," she says.

Then I send the school my acceptance.
I commit. I promise.
I plan.

And when I go to bed that night,
I dream.

Chase It

"Are you disappointed?" I ask Lindsey. "In me?"

Lindsey wraps me in a familiar hug.
"Disappointed? Yes. You would have made
a *fine* nurse, Jane. We need people like you."
She puts me at arm's length.
"Disappointed in *you*? Never. Honey,
you are my hero. Don't ever forget that.
You want to be an artist?
Go for it — that's what I say.
When you figure out what you want,
chase it, and don't let *anyone*
tell you that you shouldn't."

I'm crying a little.
"I'm going to miss you, Lindsey."
She puts her hands on her hips.
"Now, hold on. You're going to school
over in Los Angeles, right?"
I nod, snatching up a tissue.

"That means you can come home a lot.
And that means you'll visit me. Right?"
I nod again.
She goes on. "Besides, you're not going
anywhere until this fall, right?"
I blow my nose. "Right."

She relaxes. "Okay, then. In that case,
you're still mine for the next few months.
And while nursing school may not be on your agenda,
I am still going to teach you
how to *properly* wrap a bandage.
Got it? So let's not talk about good-byes
or missing each other
until we have to. Deal?"
She thrusts out her hand.
Have I mentioned I love her?
I take it, and we shake.

"Deal."

Cracked Shells

"What are these?" Justin asks,
leafing through the pile of papers
on the kitchen table.

"They're brochures for the art college
I'm going to," I tell him.
We are at my house, baking a cake.
"I wanted to show them to you."
Justin puts the pamphlets aside.
He beams. "So you'll live close by?"

"Yes, I will. Just a couple of hours away.
I will come home a *lot*."
I invite Justin to crack open the eggs.
He picks one up and studies it carefully.
"I'm glad," he tells me.
"I didn't want you to go far away."

Watching him,
I think how lucky I am,
how big the world is,
the excitement welling up inside me.
In fact, I am happier than I have been
in a good, solid year.
Going to art school? To draw and paint
and learn about art, *all day*?
I can't *wait*.

"Are *you* glad you're staying here?"
Justin asks, tapping the egg timidly
against the bowl.
The yellow insides spill out
into the batter, along with some shell.
We pick out bits of hard white.
"I'm *really* glad, Justin," I say.
"It would have been hard to leave
everyone I love too far behind."
And it would. Mom and Michael.
Justin. Mabel.
And Max. Let's not forget Max.

Justin looks at me,
those blue eyes taking everything in,
so direct and honest that it takes my breath away.
"When you finish art school,
what will you be? A mural painter?"
I put my arm around him
and squeeze his shoulders.
"I'm going to be an art teacher."

Just saying the words out loud
spreads a thrill throughout my body.
It's a choice that settled on me
at some point,
light as a butterfly,

and just as perfect.
How could I have not seen it before?
I feel like *this*
is what was meant to be.
For me.

Justin lights up.
"You'll be so *good* at that!"
He thinks a minute. Then:
"Can we paint another mural in my room
this summer? On the wall with the window?
Please?"
I laugh. "We'll ask your parents.
If they say yes, then you bet."
Taking his hand once more,
I help Justin find the right spot
on the edge of the bowl.

This time,
the egg
breaks cleanly.

Bucket List for Senior Year

✓ 1. Apply to nursing school and art college.

✓ 2. Choose one or the other.

✓ 3. Become fully certified in CPR, first aid, and triage.

✓ 4. Enter the school art competition.

5. Win the school art competition. *(Well, I tried.)*

6. Qualify for and enter the West Coast Wings art competition. *(You win some, you lose some.)*

7. Win the West Coast Wings art competition. *(Not meant to be. Turns out there were other things to reach for this year.)*

✓ 8. Go to prom.

9. Bake a wedding cake. *(Not yet, and that's fine with me. But you never know . . .)*

✓ 10. Save a life.

10. Save a Life

Cross it off my bucket list.
Not because some poor soul
choked on a hamburger
and needed the Heimlich maneuver.
Not because a bomb went off
and people were blown to bits.
(Thank goodness.)
Not because someone needed CPR,
a toe tag, or even a helping hand.
But because.

Because I made the right choice.
I know it, every single moment I am awake
(and I think even when I'm sleeping)
because
every molecule in my body *sings*
with the excitement, the pure unfettered
JOY
of a *lifetime*
with a paintbrush
in my hand.

One hand.
That's all I have.
But that's all I need.
And while it would have been
fine to become a nurse,

I believe, deep in my deepest heart,
that days would have rolled by
where I deeply regretted
parting ways with my dreams.

Sure, I may have to wait tables
or file papers or answer phones
to make ends meet until I get
my education done and find a good job.
But that's okay. It's *my* life,
and I can do what I want.

And in choosing the route
that I feel I was always —
well —
meant
to follow?
I saved a life.
And that life

is mine.

Together

Pumpkins. That's what we resemble —
pumpkins, in our orange graduation robes.
"This color makes me look so *fat*,"
Angie says, straightening her cap.
"Why can't our school have decent colors?"

"You're not fat," Michael says, dressed in shirt and tie.
"You're glowing. Like a nuclear pumpkin.
Very attractive, really."
"Michael!" Angie shrieks, faking distress.
Her father raises a camera. "Come on, everyone."
He flaps his hand at us. "Scooch together!"
We scooch, giggling as the tassels from our caps
tickle our cheeks. Mom has her camera, too.
Everyone does, and as we wrap our arms
around one another,
each camera is lifted at the same moment.
"Smile!" Elizabeth's mother says.

Today, no one needs to tell us that.
A million clicks and whizzes fill the air.

"Students, please make your way to the gymnasium,"
Principal Marks announces over the loudspeaker.
"See you in there!" I call to Mom and Michael,
who both wave, Mom kind of frantically.

"Grandma and all the rest of us
are seated on the *left*," she says. "Look for us!"
I give her a thumbs-up.

Inside we'll gather
and form our lines.
Then we'll march back outside,
to the stage,
in front of family and friends.
Then? Then it's speeches
and diplomas
and parties
and forever.

"Jane!" Justin runs from the crowd.
He is carrying the biggest trumpet-ish thing
I've ever seen.
"We got a seat in the very back,"
he says. "But I'm going to blow this
when you get up there,
so you'll know exactly where we are."

"Is that a *vuvuzela*?" I ask.
He nods proudly. "Uh-huh.
I bet you're the only person here today
who gets one of these going off for you."

"I bet you're right."
Justin squirms, but I hug him, anyway.
"Thank you."

He joins his mother,
and hand in hand, they disappear
into the crowd, Justin barely limping.

"Coming?" Rachel lags back a little.
I run to catch up, and together
we trot after Trina, Angie, and Elizabeth.

I see the school
as if seeing it for the first time.
The rafters, the bricks, the windows,
the spot where Angie and I came to terms
last year,
the spot where Max picked me up after school
last week,
the pathways I have walked
and where I have changed
and grown
over the last four years.
This school has seen me through
so much change.
And not just school, of course.
The people in it.
And today . . .

today it's over.
For real.

I guess I should be sad,
and I am . . .
but mostly?
Mostly, I'm tingling all over,
heady, giddy.
And when a loud horn squawks
in the distance, Rachel and I nudge each other
and then burst out laughing.

Next

"Jane Margaret Arrowood."

Moving toward the stage,
my legs get real stiff,
and it's like all of a sudden,
I've forgotten how to walk.
But I regain my stride
when a small roar erupts
from somewhere off to my left,
Michael's yell standing out above the mix,
and somewhere out there
that *vuvuzela* honks again and again.

"Congratulations," Principal Marks says.
He shakes my hand and holds out my diploma.
I take the scroll in hand.
Turning, I pause for the barest of seconds.
I see them — my family:
Mom, Michael, Grandma
and Uncle Ben and Aunt Karen,
and I look at the sea of faces
that makes up my classmates.
I see Rachel and Trina,
still waiting their turn.

Waving to my family,
I think, *This moment*

is a moment I'll always remember,
this instant of knowing
that I'm now
a soon-to-be college student,
a young adult,
a woman
with my whole life ahead of me,
and my hands—both of them, in my mind—
holding on firmly
to those I love.
No matter what the storms,
I will hold on.

Am I taking up my oar?
Oh, yes.
And I'm ready to paddle.

I can't wait to see
where I go next.